A Shout in the Sunshine

A Shout in the Sunshine

Mara W. Cohen Ioannides

2007 · 5767
The Jewish Publication Society
Philadelphia

The Jewish Publication Society
2100 Arch Street
Philadelphia, PA 19103
www.jewishpub.org
Cover illustration and design by Avi Katz

Manufactured in the United States of America

07 08 09 10   10 9 8 7 6 5 4 3 2 1

ISBN 13: 978-0-8276-0838-2
ISBN 10: 0-8276-0838-1

Library of Congress Cataloging-in-Publication Data

Ioannides, Mara W. Cohen.
  A shout in the sunshine / Mara W. Cohen Ioannides. -- 1st ed.
     p. cm.
  "5767."
  Summary: In fifteenth century Greece, an extraordinary friendship develops between Miguel, a refugee from post-Inquisition Spain, and David, the son of a wealthy Greek fabric merchant, despite the concerns of both Greek and Spanish Jews that the other group is not truly Jewish.
  ISBN 978-0-8276-0838-2 (alk. paper)
  1. Jews--Greece--Thessaloniki--History--15th century--Juvenile fiction. 2. Thessaloniki (Greece)--History--15th century--Juvenile fiction. [1. Jews--Greece--Thessaloniki--History--15th century--Fiction. 2. Friendship--Fiction. 3. Prejudices--Fiction. 4. Family life--Greece--Fiction. 5. Merchants--Fiction. 6. Marranos--Fiction. 7. Thessaloniki (Greece)--Fiction. 8. Greece--History--15th century--Fiction.] I. Title.

  PZ7.I5972Sho 2007
  [Fic]--dc22
                            2006033433

JPS is a nonprofit educational association and the oldest and foremost publisher of Judaica in English in North America. The mission of JPS is to enhance Jewish culture by promoting the dissemination of religious and secular works, in the United States and abroad to all individuals and institutions interested in past and contemporary Jewish life.

In memory of

PAUL SHEA COHEN

my father, my friend, my mentor
(1938–2004)

*We strive to be all that he could
imagine for us.*

Foreword

This book is about the conflict that arose in Thessalonica, commonly known as Thessaloniki, Greece, in the late 1400s and very early 1500s. The Jewish community, though small, had survived the Venetian and Ottoman claims to their part of Greece. When the Jews and Marranos were expelled from Spain in 1492 by King Ferdinand and Queen Isabella, the Ottoman Sultan Beyazit II, the ruler at this time of Thessalonica, invited the exiles to his empire, just as the existing Jewish community was raising itself out of poverty. That is not to say all were poor; rather, the community overall was. Included among these refugees were doctors, scholars, and craftsmen, who the sultan believed would only enhance the wonders of his empire. Thus, the Romaniote, or Greek, Jews had to contend with relative newcomers to their community, such as the German (Ashkenazim) and Italian (the Venetian Jews who decided to stay in the Ottoman empire) Jews—along with other groups not mentioned in this story—all of whom had different practices and interpretations of God's law. They had to clothe and house these refugees.

While some were Jewish scholars, many of these refugees knew little or nothing of Judaism. However, they all had to learn a new language, Greek, and customs while struggling with the plights of exile and poverty.

The conflict presented here is real in many respects. The existing Jewish community and the Spanish Jews had problems adapting to each other. The Spanish, Greek, Italian, and German Jews differed in many aspects of religious practice. I mentioned a few in this book, such as the betrothal ceremony and laws of butchering animals. These really had to do with interpretation of the Jewish laws. In the end, the Spanish, or Sephardic, practices became the dominant ones simply because there were many more Spanish Jews than any other community in Greece. Some of the story is fictional, like the families and their relationships. Some information is forgotten, like the design of a typical home in the city. However, the point of this story is to explore an often forgotten part of Jewish history—the Greek Jewish experience. Almost the entire Greek Jewish community was destroyed during World War II, but with the efforts of the remaining Greek community, the Greek Jewish community around the world, and scholars, the synagogues, cemeteries, and stories are slowly being saved.

Acknowledgments

A work of this kind does not just happen. Many people have played a part.

First, I must thank my daughter, Sasha, who was the inspiration. It is her mixed heritage that I am studying and passing on. She has been patient with my writing time and lavish with her enthusiastic support.

I cannot forget those who read the drafts of this and provided insight and encouragement: Sandy Asher, Linda Benson, Brenda Cohen, Ellen Fennick, Cherri Jones, and Marianthe Karanikas. Their optimism was encouraging and contagious. I cannot express the appreciation I have for my mother, who spent endless hours talking with me about ideas and helping me form the basis of this work and revise the seemingly endless drafts.

My thanks must also go to the English Department of Missouri State University. The opportunity to read a portion of this work in the Moon City Reading Series, with a number of friends playing the parts, provided a wonderful chance to receive feedback. Additionally, I must thank Missouri State University for the Faculty Research Grant that allowed me to begin my research for this book.

In addition, a number of scholars of Greek Sephardic and Romaniote history and culture offered details through either personal correspondence or their published works. Rae Dalven's and Nikos Stavroulakis's research was absolutely invaluable. *The Book of Jewish Food* by Claudia Roden was most helpful. Ken Dark's just published text *Secular Buildings and the Archaeology of Everyday Life in the Byzantine Empire* came out in the nick of time. Erika Perahia Zemour, the curator of the

Jewish Museum of Thessaloniki, was amazingly patient and helpful in finding the little details that make historical fiction so interesting.

A special thank you to my editor, Rena Potok, who has been a gentle and understanding guide through this process. Her ideas have only enhanced this book. I would also like to acknowledge the wonderful staff at JPS, who cared as much as I about getting this book "just so."

It is my hope that this book too will provide, in some manner, an historical record of a shrinking culture. The story may be fiction, but the culture and practice are factual. In this way, may the history of the Jews of Greece not be forgotten.

Chapter

1

David called out the names and colors of the bolts of fabric to his older brother Mordechai as he unloaded them.

"Black Italian wool. Orange Italian brocade. Black local wool. Janina purple silk." Mordechai checked them against his list. If a customer had requested an item, it was put aside on a corner table.

This had started as a game when David was little, every time a delivery of fabrics arrived at the store. He and his father, Hayyim, would see who was better at identifying the fabrics. Now, at 15, David was almost as tall as his father and equally as skilled. He could even tell local from Italian wool by touch. And so Hayyim no longer bothered to oversee the delivery of fabrics.

David and Mordechai had just finished when their father burst into the store. His unbuttoned feraçe billowed behind him and his arms were overloaded with material obviously just unloaded from a ship.

"Here is the list of items needed for Rebecca's dowry. This shipment is late and there are many items the women need to make before her wedding. Hurry and gather them, David, and then rush them home," he said quickly. David was not pleased with this extra chore. He still had many regular tasks to do and had thought he was finished with cataloguing the fabrics. Underneath his annoyance was a deeper feeling: he did not want his sister Rebecca to marry and move out of their father's house.

David sighed, rolled his eyes, and grunted, "Yes, Father." But Hayyim did not hear, as he was trying to decide which customer to help first. "Mordechai, I hate this."

"What is this?" his older brother asked.

"Rushing to get Rebecca married."

"David, we've talked about this," Mordechai reminded his brother, a bit annoyed. "It is not rushed. Father arranged her betrothal six months ago. Besides, a wedding is expensive for everyone, especially the bride's family. The richer the family, the more expensive the wedding. We've got two sisters: Rebecca is 14 and Rahel is already 11. I doubt Father will have paid off the debt from Rebecca's wedding before Rahel will marry."

"So what," shrugged David.

"Do you think we will walk into a betrothal and do nothing?" Mordechai asked, very perturbed. "We will have to buy gifts for our fiancées and their parents. Since Father has a good business and we will have part of it, we will need to give expensive gifts to our future in-laws."

"So what," grunted David.

Mordechai took a deep breath, squinted one eye, and said between clenched teeth, "Father could be paying off the debt for our sisters' weddings, and kiddushin, and betrothal gifts for ten years. I'll be nearly 30 before I can marry! That is ancient."

"Mordechai, you are exaggerating," retorted David.

"No, I am not," responded Mordechai. "Do you know it took Jacob bar Isaac 15 years to pay off his family's debt for his four sisters' weddings? He is almost 40! I do not want to be that old when I marry."

David looked at him coldly. "Is that all you care about? Rebecca will leave us. And then Rahel. It will not be the same anymore."

"That is life and I do not want to wait until I am old to live mine," Mordechai retorted. And with that he ended the conversation.

Hayyim was already busy with customers, having put his daughter's fabrics out of his mind. Although there was no law demanding it, Jews and Christians customarily waited to show respect until the Muslims were served, even if the Muslims had just entered the store.

Muslims were served first because the Jews, as guests in the country, felt that they should be careful not to offend their hosts in any way. A few customers milled about the store. David noticed his father helping a Muslim, distinguishable by his white turban. In one corner, three Jews stood chatting in their yellow turbans. He could not tell if they spoke the Yiddish of the Ashkenazim or the Shuadit of the Provençal Jews. Rarely did they hear Italian because the Venetian Jews were so few. As he surveyed the store noticing his unfinished jobs, an Orthodox Christian in a blue turban arrived and then left.

"David! David! Did you hear me?" Mordechai yelled in Yevanic, their mother tongue, as he shoved a package of the measured fabrics into David's arms. "Take these home to Mother and come straight back. We have many deliveries today."

Mordechai turned his head of dark curls to one of the Ashkenazic customers who was looking for a piece of fabric. He switched to speaking Yiddish.

While David was good with fabric, Mordechai was good with languages. "Fabric for a Torah mantle? A mantle like a coat? For your wife to embroider in honor of your twins' good health. Mazel tov on their birth and your wife's recovery. May they live to be married …. But the Torah is kept in a tik, not a fabric mantle, no?"

David was pondering how a Torah mantle would look as he left the store carrying the large bundle. He knew that Jews from different parts of the world had different customs, but a coat for a Torah seemed strange. How flimsy! In only a cloth wrapping, the wind and rain could possibly touch the holy scrolls; without a doubt, a tik was better. A solid case of wood painted or covered in silver protected the scrolls from all weather.

Just outside the shop door, he bumped into a poorly dressed boy his own age. His clothes were almost impossible to identify. The shirt and trousers were too small for the boy and were gray from wear and age, so David did not notice in his haste that they were of a foreign style. As he passed, David absent mindedly yelled at him in Greek to watch where he was going. The boy looked up in surprise, bowed in apology, and entered the store.

Even though the house and store connected to each other, David's grandfather had built a wall between them so that one had to go around the block to enter the house. It kept thieves from looting both the store and the house at the same time. David practically ran around the block, and rushed through the front door and entrance hall to the courtyard where his mother, sisters, aunts, and female cousins were gathered, gossiping and embroidering Rebecca's dowry. He did not speak, but dropped at the feet of his grandmother, simply because he saw her first, a large bundle of fabric. Then he turned and left, almost stepping on a baby that had crawled in front of him.

His mother beamed with pride, "Finally, the shipment of fabrics has arrived and we can complete the dowry. The store must be busy if David does not have time to say hello. Come let us see what my husband has sent."

Rebecca was excited. They were all there to honor her. Today, the entire group had gathered to help complete her dowry. Rebecca had received coins from Jacob and his mother, and her father had ordered a chest that contained some silver objects. Now that they had the fabrics, they could finish Rebecca's clothes. Rebecca was excited to pick through the fabrics her father had sent.

"Manna, look at the brocades. A peach and rose, green and blue. Papa sent beautiful things!" she cried with joy. She and her cousins and sister, Rahel, started deciding which fabrics would work best for which item in her dowry.

"Rebecca, sit with us," suggested an aunt. "You are the guest of honor. There is no need to trouble yourself with those fabrics."

"No, thank you, Thea," replied Rebecca as she continued. "Yaiya, are you sure that the quilt is stuffed enough?" she asked her grandmother. Her mind was a whirl of details and she felt terribly grown-up. All these items to finish. Thank heaven all of her family was there to help. If only they would do it all the way she wanted them to. Every person had to explain why his or her way was better, the design prettier, or the talisman more effective. As fun as this was, it was also terribly tedious.

"Child, what do you know about quilts? I have made more than you are old," replied her grandmother, Rahel, gently.

At that moment Hadassah arrived from the kitchen with a tray of goodies. She came into the courtyard like a mighty force.

"Rahel, keep Rachamim out of the bag of feathers. Mother, are you supervising the quilt? Where is Miriam? There you are. Have you finished embroidering the tablecloth?" These questions rolled out of her mouth without a pause between them, so quickly that it was impossible to answer one before the next was asked.

"Daughter, sit and rest," recommended her mother. "This will all be done in good time. Look, Rebecca has finished embroidering Jacob's tallit case so that his prayer shawl will be safe. She has also done a beautiful job on her belt." Her grandmother winked at her.

Rebecca smiled. Compliments from her grandmother were rare. It helped to make up for some of her disappointment. She had two new pairs of nalin as part of the dowry. For a week after these new shoes had been ordered, Rebecca had cried to herself. Desperately, she wanted the bright colored ones she had seen peeking out from under the feraçe of Muslim women at the market, but it was forbidden by law. Jews had to wear black. Her mother had pointed out that they really were more like overshoes since they were worn over one's soft-soled leather boots to protect the leather from the mud of the streets. The quality of her boots and the beauty of her outfits were therefore more important. That did little to mollify Rebecca, until now. On this beautiful day, everyone was here admiring her dowry, and helping to complete it. Her outfits were going to be gorgeous, perhaps more beautiful than any one else's.

"Steroulla, I'm thrilled with the match Hayyim made for Rebecca," commented her grandmother to her mother. "An important scholar from a good middle-class family." Hadassah smiled at her mother. Only she still used the pet name Steroulla.

"Yes. Kyrio Jacob bar Isaac is a distant cousin of my husband's and his family is a good one," replied Hadassah distractedly, less concerned at the moment with Kyrio Jacob than with the hungry group of women she had to feed.

Grandmother Rahel looked up from Rachamim, her littlest grandchild, who squirmed in her lap, "Steroullaki, Rebecca is a good girl. You have brought her up to keep a kosher home and take care of her husband and family. Your husband is a good man and we all know he has chosen carefully for his first daughter, just as he will for his second." At the end of this statement, she spat three times on the floor to ward off the evil eye.

Rahel looked up in concern. Her grandmother had mentioned a husband for her. She was only 11, what nonsense. She quickly pushed the idea from her mind as she returned to the fabrics. Every scrap, no matter how small, she wanted. What wonderful clothes she could make for her dolls.

Chapter

2

David ran back to the store to find the two Jews still waiting; he had only been gone a few minutes. He spent the day climbing ladders to find bolts of fabrics on high shelves and following customers home with their deliveries. Finally, the store was empty.

Hayyim, Mordechai, and David sat and rested. Too tired to even talk, they just stared at each other. At this moment, the boy David had bumped into earlier in the day came into the store and approached them, speaking in a language they did not recognize. The three stared at him and then each other in disbelief. How could this be? They were all fluent in Yevanic, Greek, and Arabic, and knew enough Yiddish, Shuadit, and Italian to do business with their customers. Maybe, each thought, he was simply too tired to understand.

The boy, dark haired with green eyes, tried again, this time in broken Greek. "Good ... evening, good men. I sad to break your ... talk at the end of the day, but I see you were busy and did not want to break your early talk."

Mordechai interrupted, "What is it you want? We are very tired." While he was good with the customers, Mordechai had no patience for beggars, and this boy looked like a beggar. His frail body and raggedy clothes disgusted Mordechai. It was impossible at this point of the day for him even to feign politeness.

"I see you ... busy. You could use some help?" the boy said humbly and quietly. He hung his head and did not look at any of the three.

Now Hayyim jumped in, "Are you seeking an apprenticeship? Have you no father or uncle to speak for you?" Hayyim thought it impertinent of the boy to come on his own; there were proper ways to

7

conduct business. And yet, there was something about the boy's manner that kept Hayyim from throwing him out immediately.

"I have no father or uncle," the boy said unabashedly as he looked at Hayyim. "My older … cousin is a low assistant in a silver shop and does not … have time to come and speak." Inside the boy quaked, but outside he showed no sign of it. He knew it was rude for him to come alone; however, he had no choice.

"What is the language you first spoke? And what is your name?" asked Hayyim, examining him closely. Hayyim was curt, but he had a soft heart. It was clear to him that this boy, because of the way he stood, was no mere beggar. Despite his humility, he stood straight and with an air of confidence that implied he was a member of an important family.

"I am called Miguel Vide and my language is Spanish," came the response with a polite nod of his head.

David sat up straight, suddenly fascinated. A Spanish Jew! They had never met one before. The Spanish community had arrived in Thessaloniki only a few months earlier. At least now they understood why the boy's language seemed familiar; they had heard it in the streets and at the market. In fact, it was everywhere. The refugees from Spain had overwhelmed the city. The language was vaguely like Shuadit or French, but because they had never had a Spaniard as a customer, they had never actually heard the language.

"Miguel, return tomorrow at the end of the day and we shall have an answer for you," Hayyim replied with a wave of his hand in dismissal—he was too tired to think. Then Hayyim ran that same hand through his beard, straightened his vest, and stood up. He turned to Mordechai, "You can do the books tomorrow, Mordechai. It is late. Let us go home." As they closed up the store, Miguel slipped out. None of them took notice.

That evening as the three men ate their supper, they discussed Miguel. They sat on low cushions around a low table upon which was spread an array of dishes. They spooned food from the dishes onto the plates in front of them. As they talked, they grabbed the food with their fingers and carefully raised it to their mouths. Each had rolled his right sleeve up and tucked it under so as not to dirty it as he ate. There was no concern about the left sleeve because no one ate with his left hand. The Muslim rulers believed the left hand to be dirty, and so now the Jews did, too.

"I do not like the idea of hiring a Spaniard," began Hayyim. "What do we know of his family? Is he really Jewish or like those … ," and he paused here to find the foreign word, "Marranos who claim they were Christians only by day?" Hayyim was impressed with Miguel's forthrightness, but he was also concerned about maintaining his prosperous business. Customers were not only concerned with the quality of the cloth; they were also concerned with the quality of the merchant.

"But father," interjected David, "Miguel Vide must be a Jew. He says he is. There are many Spanish-speaking Jews in the city now and if we had someone who could speak Spanish …"

At this moment their mother walked in with another tray of food.

"What kind of name is Miguel Vide?" she asked. "We know who we are by our fathers' names: Hayyim bar David bar Isaac bar Joseph. What name is Vide?" In most families, women's voices were not thought to be important unless they were speaking about family matters, but Hayyim had great respect for his wife and so she could ask such a question. He found Hadassah to be not only beautiful, but also wise. Her advice about business matters was often correct and she was an excellent judge of people. However, her knowledge of world affairs was minimal, which was not surprising since she had few contacts with anyone, especially men, outside their community.

He answered her gently but not patronizingly, "The Spanish have a name for the whole family which passes from one generation to the next. They do not use their fathers' names as we do." Then he returned to the consuming conversation with his sons, "The Spanish do not have great wealth any longer and will learn to speak Greek. We may need help in the store, but we have never hired outside the Romaniote community. I see no point in doing so now." Hayyim was conservative about his business and he spoke with a finality he was not sure he believed.

David was undeterred, "Father, the number of Spanish Jews is amazing! You hear the language everywhere. How can we not learn it?"

Mordechai turned on his brother, "We will never hire outside the community. How do we even know this … this Miguel is Jewish? I've heard that even the refugees argue this point—who among them is Jewish. There are some who are called Marranos, who were secret Jews and the Sephardim question their beliefs."

At that moment Rachamim toddled into the room toward his father. His chubby face was all smiles when he saw his father and brothers look at him. He started to run, tripped over his feet, and landed on the floor.

"Mimi, Mimi-aki," called Rahel from just down the hall." Why are you crying?" she demanded as she dashed into the room. She cooed as she picked him up. Rahel was in charge of Mimi, as the family called him. "I'm sorry father. We should not disturb your supper," she said as she brushed Mimi's knees and gave him a kiss on his forehead.

"That is fine, children. Rahel go play. Mimi can stay and eat with us," commented Hayyim as he wiped his hand on the napkin draped over his knee, before he grabbed his youngest and sat him on his other knee. Rahel was not hard to persuade. As much as she loved her baby brother, there were times when she wished she did not have to take care of him. She considered herself lucky, though, because a number of her cousins had to watch two or three younger siblings. Rahel gleefully kissed her father and dashed off to find her dolls. Rachamim climbed onto his father's lap and picked at the various plates, as his father carefully wiped his son's hands. David tried to convince Hayyim to hire Miguel and Hayyim resisted. There was something about Miguel that resonated in David; something in that other boy intrigued him. Finally, David found a way to make Hayyim think his way.

"Father, what if I was Miguel? What if I had no father to teach me business and I had to travel to a foreign land alone?" Hayyim and

Mordechai stared at him. When had he thought of such an idea? Mimi munched on a piece of bread while sitting in his father's lap.

David opened his mouth to continue, but Hayyim interrupted, suddenly inspired. "When did you become so wise, my son? Jews should help Jews. The Muslims do not understand the differences among us. They see us all as Jews, not as Spanish, Greek, German, or Venetian. They do not understand that our practices are different, our traditions are different, and our languages are different. Even though he is a bit old, we'll hire Miguel as a helper, an apprentice. He will do the deliveries and unload the shipments."

Mordechai argued, "But we have no proof he is even Jewish! And how will we communicate?" But his father brushed him away with a wave of his hand.

David was ecstatic! He grinned at his father, then jumped up and ran and hugged him. Now, he could find out more about this community of refugees he had heard so much about. In addition, he would not be doing all the work associated with an apprentice. He could do something more adult.

Mordechai slumped back in his cushions. He did not like the idea of hiring a stranger, especially one who barely spoke their language and certainly did not know their customs. This Miguel could be embarrassing. He could drive away customers with his bad breath, or ignore a Muslim and help a Christian.

David's mother returned to clear the table. Mimi cried when the dishes were removed; he was still hungry. Then Rebecca came in with her sewing and Rahel with her toys, and the family enjoyed a quiet hour or two. There were no visitors this evening, so the family could spend time together telling stories, playing, and singing. When there were guests, the women excused themselves to a different room.

After the children had gone to sleep, Hayyim lay in bed with Hadassah and discussed the prospective new employee.

"We could use some help in the store," he half whispered. "David is really getting too old to do the work normally done by an apprentice.

Besides we are far too busy for him to be running around town with deliveries."

Hadassah was adamantly against hiring a Spaniard.

"We have never hired anyone outside the family," she retorted.

"Hadassah, I cannot remember a time that we have ever hired anyone," Hayyim replied. "But I need help and there will be a time when I can no longer work in the store. I need to train Mordechai."

Hadassah took a deep breath.

"I do not like the idea of hiring an outsider—someone we do not know," she said huffily and turned over.

Hayyim put his arm around her.

"You just do not like change, kooklia. There is, however, something this boy has that none of us do."

Hadassah turned over in surprise and asked, "What?"

"A knowledge of Spanish, dearest," was his reply. "There are many Spanish Jews, some with money and the rest will have money soon enough. We need to work with these people."

Hadassah pondered this for a moment.

"Are there really that many Spanish now?" she asked.

"Absolutely," Hayyim said to the darkness.

"Then," she replied quietly, "I guess we will hire this boy if for no other reason than to have him teach Mordechai and David Spanish." Thus, they reached an accord in the darkness.

Chapter

3

David was excited to be at work the next day. He wanted to
meet Miguel again—a Spanish Jew! He had often heard
them talked about in the synagogue. Some of what he had heard was
true, some was false, but which was which was hard to tell. The parts
he knew were true were told by the Millet Bashi in the synagogue. Ferdinand, the Christian king of Spain, had exiled these refugees because
they were Jews. The sultan of the Ottoman Empire, Beyazit II, had
invited these Jews to live in his lands. They were supposed to be smart,
doctors and scholars; why then was Miguel so poor? Why did he not
have a father or uncle? There were so many questions. The day went by
slowly. David kept stopping and looking down the street. Where was
Miguel?

As David was sweeping the shop at the end of the day, Miguel
appeared at the door.

"I thought you were not coming," commented David without
giving away any of his excitement. "Go in and see my father." David
longed to join the conversation, but he knew his place and that his
chores had to be finished before evening prayers. That, however, did
not keep him from listening. He swept as quietly as he could. Once, he
realized his broom had stopped and he quickly started sweeping again.

"Excuse me," interrupted Miguel quietly, in broken Greek, as he
approached David's father. "I have come back." He was nervous and excited. All day he had barely been able to contain himself. He did not
tell anyone in his family about his request for work, not his cousin,
aunt, grandmother, or even his sister in whom he confided everything. They had very little money, as they were surviving on his

cousin's income as an apprentice. Any money he earned would significantly change their lives. There seemed no point in raising their hopes. Better not to disappoint them if he did not get the job. To hide his anxiety, he had spent the day at the wharf. Although he could control his body, his voice and eyes betrayed him. His voice cracked and his eyes darted around the room afraid to focus on the man in front of him.

"I see you speak some Greek," said Hayyim sharply. "That is good. It will improve with time. And you are to make sure my sons learn Spanish." Miguel grinned. "Do not get too excited. Bring your cousin—he is the man of the family, yes?—bring him to my house after evening prayers and we will sign a contract." With that Hayyim turned his back on Miguel and returned to the accounts with Mordechai. He saw no reason to become familiar with this boy or to encourage his enthusiasm.

"Gracias, Señor," responded Miguel. He turned to leave and saw David standing in the doorway, "Tell me, little Señor, where is your house?"

David laughed. Everyone knew where the house of Hayyim bar David was; he was as wealthy and as powerful in the community as any Romaniote Jew, as any Jew.

Without turning around, Mordechai called out, "David, do not be rude." No matter how he felt about his father's decision rudeness was inexcusable, especially now that this boy was an employee. Mordechai made a mental note to teach David this too: hide your feelings and smile to everyone. That was what a businessman did.

David shook his head to clear the laughter and explained as he pointed to the shop entrance, "Walk around to the back of the store. The entrance is opposite this door." Holding the smile inside, he returned to his work. Miguel bowed again and fairly danced out the door.

As he flew down the street, Miguel's thoughts whirled. Another income! There would be a celebration at his house tonight. Meat for dinner; perhaps new clothes. He could not go to work in these rags. How proud everyone would be. Tía Maria would give him a big hug, just as she used to when their tutor praised his schoolwork. Miguel could see the sparkle in his sister Clara's eyes. Maybe his cousin José would smile again.

Evening was falling and so Miguel ran straight to the synagogue, where he and his cousin José prayed. The synagogue was known to everyone as the Spanish Expulsion because it was founded by the Sephardim. Evening prayers had not yet begun and Miguel danced among the crowd of men speaking Ladino and Spanish until he found José. For many of those in attendance, evening prayer was as much about seeing each other and catching up on the day's news, as it was about praying. For many, like Miguel and José, joining in the evening prayers was also a way to learn about Judaism and to learn the prayers themselves.

"José! José!" he tugged on his cousin's sleeve. "We go to Señor Hayyim's tonight. He said I could work in his store." Miguel's eyes were ablaze with triumph.

José looked down at his cousin. He was more than fond of the boy. After all, he was more than Miguel's cousin; he was his friend and brother and father. José was only five years older than Miguel, but he had always been more responsible. Their fathers had been brothers and José remembered them both. It was clear to everyone that the two were related. They had the same dark wavy hair and green eyes. Miguel and his sister had been orphaned before they could really remember their parents. So José felt quite protective of his cousins.

"You are incorrigible, sneaking off to find yourself a job. That is quite improper," he said with a grin. "Let us pray and then we'll go. No! First we must tell Abuela." She was the matriarch.

"No, José. Señor said right after prayers," responded Miguel. "Let us surprise Abuela and Tía Maria with the news." José was about to respond when the prayers began. After the prayers, they compromised. Señor Juan Abravanel lived next door; he would stop in to tell their grandmother they had business and would be home late.

At the Vides' house, Clara was busy setting the table, so that dinner would be ready when her brother and cousin returned from prayers. Despite the Muslim custom of separation of the sexes, the Vide family maintained the Spanish tradition of the family dining together. Her aunt was watching the food cooking on the cook stove in the corner of the room. Her grandmother sat by the window watching the people go by through the gaps in the ornate shutters. Ottoman rule demanded that women be carefully hidden, something that all the Vide women were struggling with, as were their fellow exiles, and looking through the carvings in the shutter was the only way that Teresa could view the street. It was peaceful, something Teresa and Maria appreciated after a lifetime of living in fear and secrecy. Although remaining behind physical shutters was difficult, it was in many ways easier than the emotional shutters they had lived behind in Spain.

Suddenly, a strong knock on the door broke the peace. The two women looked at each other nervously—could it be soldiers?

"How silly we are," commented Teresa Vide. "We are in a peaceful place. There are no soldiers or priests to fear here. Daughter-in-law, answer the door." Maria gracefully crossed the room and opened the door, as her mother-in-law requested.

There stood their neighbor Señor Abravanel. It was rare that he called on them. Usually, his young wife Eva, only a few years older than Clara, came over to seek advice or company. She bore a heavy burden of taking care of her husband Juan, their baby, Juan's youngest brother (who was not much older than she), and her own brother. Like many Marranos, she had no other family to rely on and turned to these neighbors for help. Tonight, however, it was Señor Abravanel at their door.

Immediately, Señora Vide became concerned, "Señor Abravanel, what brings you to our home at this hour?"

"Señora," said Juan as he bowed to the older woman, "and Señora, and Señorita," he added with a smile as he bowed to the other two, "it is not bad news so calm yourselves. Your grandsons asked that I stop in on my way home to let you know that they had some business to do and would be home later than usual."

"Business so late?" asked Maria concerned. "Do you know what business?"

Juan turned to look at the proud woman.

"I'm afraid they did not say, though Miguel could barely contain his excitement. They should be home shortly. Now, if you'll excuse me, I must return to Señora Eva and my family." With that he bowed to the three women, grasped the door handle, and backed out of the room shutting the door as he went.

This genteel gesture made Maria smile wistfully.

"How much like the Spanish courtiers who visited my family when I was a child," she commented mostly to herself.

Clara looked at her aunt with shining eyes, "Tía Maria, what do you think José and Miguel are doing? Do you think they'll have a surprise for us?"

Señora Vide looked at her granddaughter sharply, "A surprise? And what surprise do you think two poor men like them could afford?" With that she turned to Maria, "Our greater concern is supper. Should we wait or eat without them?"

Maria pondered this question for a moment.

"Let us wait a bit," she replied. "The soup certainly will not burn. And should we get hungry we can always eat then. They'll understand."

"Come here, Clara," called Teresa. "Let us begin your lessons early this evening. I want you to have the same education as your mother, aunt, and myself. We must review some history, politics, and mathematics. If only we still had a lute," she regretfully declared. "Never mind, your singing is quite good. I will not have you ignorant like the local women. Their knowledge of Judaism may be stronger, but since they cannot read, their minds are filled with superstitions." The two sat down near the window. "Let us begin with a song, Clara," commanded Teresa, "Sing 'A la una nasi yo (At one I was born).'"

Clara took a breath, "Oh, I love this song! It reminds me of…beautiful things." And she began:

A la una nasi yo,	*At one I was born,*
A laz dos me baptizaron,	*At two they baptized me;*
A laz tres despozi yo,	*At three I was betrothed,*
Ninya de mi korason.	*Child of my heart.*
Ninya de mi korason.	*Child of my heart.*

17

A laz kwatro me kazaron,	At four I was married,
Me kaszi kon un amore	I wed with a love—
Alma i vida i korason	Soul, life and heart.
Lo moreno izo el Dio	God creates the dark beauty,
Lo blanko izo el platero	The artist (silversmith), the blond beauty.
Biva la djenté morena	Long live dark beauties (brunettes)
Ke por eyos bivo yo.	For whom I live—soul, life, and heart.
Ke por eyos bivo yo.	For whom I live—soul, life, and heart.
Biva la djenté morena	Long live the dark beauties (people),
Ke por eyoz mwero yo	For them I die;
Alma i vida i korason.	Soul, life, and heart.
Di mi, ninya, d'onde vyenez?	Tell me young woman, where do you come from?
Ke te kero konoser;	I would like to know you,
I sit u tyenez amante	And if you have a love
Yo to are prentender.	I will court you.
Yo to are prentender.	I will court you.
I si no tyenez amante.	And if you do not have a love
Yo te are defender	I will be your defender,
Alma i vida i korason.	Soul, life, and heart.

When she finished each woman was silent listening to the song in her own heart and reliving moments from her past life in Spain.

After a while, Maria called the other two to the table, "Come Clara, come Mother, it is late. We will eat and then wait for the boys." The three sat around the table with its unmatched bowls and creaky stools and ate their soup. Teresa could not adjust to sitting on cushions on the floor; she insisted upon at least stools. Then Clara washed the bowls and put them away on the mantle shelf.

Chapter

4

After asking Juan to deliver the message, Miguel and José left the gate of the synagogue and headed toward the Romaniote neighborhood.

"Where is the place, Miguel?" asked José. He rarely left the few blocks surrounding the room they rented. He went from home, to work, to pray, to home. There was time for little else.

Miguel led him through the various Jewish neighborhoods, until they reached the Romaniote one. While the buildings were not very different from other neighborhoods, it all seemed new and unusual. They marched past a vendor selling flaky pastries filled with meat or spinach. Men, boys, and girls filled the streets. A few grown women glided by with at least one servant. Some serving women walked alone. They were easy to distinguish from their ladies because their feraçes were faded and patched. José had no time to ponder any of these things because they were suddenly standing in front of a door and Miguel was knocking.

Inside, David was walking by the door when he heard knocking. He opened it wide. There stood Miguel with a grown man. The man's age was hard to guess—his eyes looked old, but his face was young. It was clear from their features they were related.

David remembered his manners, "Come in Miguel and…"

Miguel jumped right in, "José Vide, my cousin."

"Yes, your cousin. My father is expecting you. Please follow me." David showed Miguel and José into the formal room.

Hayyim sat on an ornate couch waiting. His white hair was combed and clothes neat, but his beard betrayed his emotions with finger marks where he had stroked it. David brought the well-stuffed cushions for their guests to sit upon. José noted their status. Hayyim's power was represented by his height and comfort and their low status as relatively unimportant visitors by their place.

Rahel had heard the knock at the door and hid out of sight behind a plant in the courtyard, so she could watch David walk the two men to the formal room. Curious about who these guests were, she devised a plan to find out. As she and Mimi played in the courtyard, she slowly inched her way toward the formal room.

"Rahel, be careful with that ball," cautioned her mother, both quietly and sternly, as she passed with a tray of treats. While it was usual for Hadassah to provide hospitality at a business meeting, Dinah, the servant woman, usually brought in the tray, allowing Hadassah to maintain her modesty. However, Hadassah wanted to find out about these foreigners, so this evening she brought the tray herself. Hadassah was careful to keep her eyes downcast, but this did not keep her from seeing what these guests looked like. Rahel knew her mother's practices and so was doubly curious. She followed her mother. She leaned against the doorframe hidden among the shadows so that she could hear without being seen. Her youth meant that it was not forbidden for non-family members to see her, but the one thing her father was very strict about was the modesty and propriety of his women. Her duties to Rachamim were forgotten with the excitement of these unknown visitors.

David thought it best to begin since his father looked uncomfortable. "This is José Vide, Miguel's cousin."

"Kyrio Vide, your cousin came to me seeking employment," began Hayyim. "It is true our store is a busy place, sometimes too busy, and help would be good. However, it is rare we turn to strangers."

"But father, they are not truly strangers," interrupted David, who immediately realized he had said the wrong thing. A son never corrects his father, especially not publicly in front of strangers. Despite what he had said to his father, these men were strangers. They did not know these Sephardim or their families; José carried no letter of introduction. Unfortunately, there was no appropriate way to get out of the mistake.

His father saved him, although he sent a sharp look David's way. "David is right. Jews are never strangers to fellow Jews, but we know nothing of your family, your background."

There was silence in the room as José pondered this comment. "I can speak to you only what I know. Our family are Marranos, secret Jews."

A hiss was heard in the doorway. The four men turned to see Hayyim's wife, Hadassah, carrying a tray of refreshments. Hayyim gave her a stern look and returned his attention to José's story.

"Our grandparents claimed Catholicism to save ... their lives, but they never ... followed in their hearts ... and prayed at night in ... closets and cellars as Jews. My grandmother ... she tell me that my Papa was to ... teach me the secrets of Jews on my thirteenth year, but he disappeared when I was ten. Miguel and Clara, his young sister, come to us when they were tiny. I remember Miguel father, my father brother, only ... a little bit ... but I do remember the children coming to our house. A weeping servant bring them to my grandmother in the dark of the night. She kept saying: 'the inquisitor, the inquisitor.' She left as quickly as she could and we never see her again. My parents raise Miguel and Clara as my brother and sister. When my Papa not come home ... my Mama keep us all together. Now we have only Grandmother and Mama."

Rebecca came down the hall and saw Rahel listening in at the door.

Something interesting must be happening, she thought, so she stood behind Rahel and listened. It did not occur to her the danger she was in. If her father discovered her in a place where a man who was not a relative might see her uncovered, she would be severely punished. The mystery of the moment was too overwhelming. Mordechai saw his sisters and snuck up behind them to find out what was so interesting.

Slowly, Hadassah put down the tray of pickled vegetables and rosewater tea on the low table. Not only did she not want to disturb the men, but also she did not want them to notice her so that she could remain longer in the room. David suddenly realized the house was quiet except for Dinah, their servant, banging pots in the kitchen. Where were the sounds of Mimi running and Rahel shouting after him? What of Rebecca's endless calls of " Manna" as she scurried around the house? Then he did hear Mimi running, although Mimi did not come into the room, which was his usual practice. In fact, Mimi bumped into Mordechai, which caused Mordechai's arm to bump Rebecca, and Rebecca's hair flew across her face and tickled her nose. She sneezed. Rahel looked around sharply, gave her siblings a nasty look, and then refocused on the conversation in the formal room. The three siblings all stood quietly. Mordechai held Rachamim in his arms to keep him quiet. Very slowly and quietly, David's mother backed away from the men.

José continued, "My grandfather was a wealthy man—a money lender. My Papa and uncle get the business when he died, but did not do well. Grandmother says it is because the Catholics refused to buy their … things again. They would threaten to take my Papa and uncle to court. The Catholic courts … never help Jews or new Catholics, those from Jewish families. When Miguel's Mama and Papa get disappeared, the business got badder and often my Papa stay at home. I remember furniture, rugs, and silver going from the house, and then the servants go. When my Papa disappeared, Mama and Grandmother sold many of what was left to buy him back, but it did no good. By the time we were forced to leave by King Ferdinand, the only thing left was the house. Grandmother spent all that she got for selling it on our trip here."

When José finished the story each person in the room was lost in his own thoughts. Miguel learned his family had been wealthy when he was little and that his parents had not abandoned them, but had been taken from him. He tried hard to remember their faces, but failed. David was glad he had convinced his father to have Miguel and José in the house. He was the first of his friends to meet and entertain a Spanish Jew. Would not his cousins be envious when he told them tomorrow at evening prayers? Rahel was mesmerized by the story. How could people disappear and leave their children? Where did those people go? What happened to them? Rebecca wanted to know who were these men in the formal room and why were they there (she had missed the beginning of the meeting). Mordechai had remained focused on the idea of being a Christian by day and a Jew by night. How could people divide their loyalties like that? He wanted to know which they truly were.

Hayyim spoke carefully changing his mind on the hiring of Miguel. He knew that not only was his whole family listening (he had been aware of their eavesdropping throughout the meeting) but also he was making a statement on behalf of the entire community. "José Vide of Thessaloniki," he said, "I cannot hire your cousin, Miguel Vide of Thessaloniki, as an apprentice." Immediately, the cousins turned white and José began to rise, pulling Miguel up with him. Hayyim waved at him to sit. "I cannot hire him as an apprentice, because I would like to hire him as an assistant. He certainly does not need to be trained how to work with people and stock shelves. We will try him for three months and then discuss a permanent position."

From the hall came an approving yelp and then Rahel, in her best imitation of a mature woman said, "Mimi, do not step on my foot again." Everyone but Mordechai broke into grins. He had been stuck behind his sisters and mother, and burst into the room with a concerned look on his face. While he empathized with this family's plight, hiring an employee outside of the family meant that a portion of the income the store provided would leave the family. How could his father let this happen? Their taxes to the Ottoman rulers were high and who knew how long their prosperity would last? When this sultan died, the next one might not be as generous to his Jewish subjects.

Yet, it seemed at that moment that Mordechai was the only one with concerns and misgivings. Rebecca was not sure why she was so happy. She did not care much about her father's business except that it meant she dressed very well because her father let her have whatever she liked from the store, as long as it was within the sultan's dress codes. Perhaps, she thought, it is because everyone else is pleased. And these men look so poor and pitiful.

Rahel was intrigued. The men had traveled to many exotic places; what stories they had to tell. She eagerly looked forward to hearing them.

David knew he would be the envy of his cousins; he was going to learn Spanish from a real Spaniard.

Now that their business was complete, Hayyim invited José and Miguel to share the treats on the tray his wife had brought. The two cousins graciously accepted, but stayed only as long as custom demanded, because they had to hurry home to bring the good news to their family.

Two hours after Juan Abravanel left, the boys burst into the room. Miguel practically exploded with the news, "Tía Maria, Abuela, it is truly wonderful!"

José was trying to contain himself and act his twenty years, "Miguel, that is not the way to tell such important news. Mother, bring us our dinner and join us at the table, and we'll tell you the story," he commanded with an authoritarian tone. With that the two threw themselves onto stools at the table. Maria brought each a bowl of soup and the three ladies joined them. The men practically dove into the bowls. After a few spoonfuls, José began, "Abuela, Mother, Clara," and here he paused for effect, "Miguel has a job."

Maria clasped her hands. "Dios mio! Tell me, my sons, about this job. For whom will you be an apprentice, Miguel?" Though Miguel was her nephew, she had raised him since he was young and considered Miguel and Clara as her own son and daughter.

Miguel grinned at his cousin and then looked at his aunt, "Tía Maria, I will not be an apprentice. Señor Hayyim bar David, who owns a busy cloth business, has hired me as an assistant in the store. And he called me Miguel Vide of Thessaloniki. Of Thessaloniki! Can you imagine?"

A gasp went among the three women. Everyone was silent for a moment contemplating this statement. A leader of the Romaniote community had made it known that the Vides were citizens of Thessaloniki—they were no longer refugees.

Finally, Señora Vide asked carefully, "Miguel, what do we know of these people? Who are his customers?"

"Abuela, I sat near his shop all day. There were Christians and Muslims, and Jews who spoke Shuadit, Italian, and Greek, but no Spanish. His sons work there. One is my age! The people respect him and he treats them kindly."

"My little grandson, what kind of Jews are they?" repeated the matriarch, her face darkening.

"They are Romaniote," replied her grandson quietly. There was silence in the room.

Señora Vide said softly, "They may have been helpful once, but recently they have turned cold, even resentful of our presence. The Provençals, Venetians, and Ashkenazim tolerate us at least."

"But Abuela," interjected Clara, "he said Miguel was a citizen. How is that unkind?"

"Child, while one person can claim we are citizens, the entire community must agree to it. He will be swayed by the other Romaniotes," was her grandmother's sad reply.

"José," Maria turned to her son, "this family will treat Miguel fairly?"

"Yes, Mother," replied José with conviction. "We have signed a contract of work. Miguel will be paid to deliver merchandise and clean the store. He will help when needed and teach the sons, David and Mordechai, Spanish. Señor Hayyim was impressed that Miguel speaks Arabic and wants him to learn better Greek."

"Good," said Maria. "You have done well. Finish your soup, my boys. I will return shortly." She wrapped herself in her feraçe and left the room.

While she was gone, Clara peppered the boys with questions, "What did the house look like? What did they wear? Were there girls? What foods were you fed?"

"Clara, stop!" commanded José. "I can only answer one question at a time. And the answers are all—I do not know."

"How can you not know?" Clara moaned. "You were there. Was it a big house with many servants? Was it small? Were there paintings on the walls?"

Miguel stopped her. "Clara, we were there on business. We did not stop and gawk. That would make it seem like we had never been invited to anyone's house before. We did not study the walls or the patterns on the plates. Now, let me eat my dinner in peace."

Clara was sullen. How could they not have noticed? Silently, internally, she bewailed the fact that she never had the chance to visit outside their community. She would have noticed without being noticed, the kinds of food they were offered, what everyone wore, the patterns on the dishes, and the subjects of the art on the walls. How frustrating her brother and cousin could be sometimes.

When Maria returned twenty minutes later, she carried a cloth containing sweets.

"Come everyone," she commanded, "a small treat to celebrate the family's good fortune." They gathered around the table again to feast on a rarely offered dessert.

Chapter

5

That night, Rebecca and Rahel lay in their bed. "Rahel," asked Rebecca with a touch of annoyance, "did you wipe your feet before you climbed in? There is grit in the bed."

"I thought I did," replied Rahel. "Pull back the quilt and I'll brush the bed off."

Rebecca did as her sister requested. As she watched the glowing outline of Rahel bend over with the backlight of the moon as it shone through the shutter, she asked, "What is the fuss over hiring this new assistant for the store?"

Rahel smoothed the quilt as she lay down. She was thankful that the room was dark so that Rebecca would not see her annoyance. As much as she loved her sister, her ignorance of anything outside of housekeeping could get very frustrating.

Rahel took a deep breath, "The Spanish are new here and many people fear new things."

"Why did they come here and make trouble?" asked Rebecca petulantly. Her joy for Miguel and his family had been forgotten as her distrust and immaturity overtook her.

"They are guests of the sultan," responded Rahel crossly. "From what I have heard their sultan exiled them because they refused to stop being Jews."

Now Rebecca was confused, "If they refused to stop being Jews, why does Manna question if they are Jews?"

Rahel took a deep breath and let it out with a long sigh.

"Did you not listen to Kyrio José's story?" she asked in frustration. "They pretended not to be Jews. If they do that, how will they understand Judaism? They are Jews by birth, but are they Jews by practice?"

Rebecca yawned, "Does it matter? They have come and made trouble and I do not like it." With that, she turned over. Her thoughts, as she fell asleep, were on the chores she had for tomorrow. Any news outside of family interests rarely remained long on her mind. It seemed to her as though each day her mother made her do even more. How she longed for the chance to stay in the courtyard and play, like Rahel. And so she fell asleep.

"But Rebecca," began her sister, "do you not care that they are exiled? How sad it must be for them." There was no answer. Rebecca was asleep. Rahel sighed again. As usual, her sister did not care to know the truth. While Rebecca's concern was homemaking and family care, Rahel was far more interested in the world outside. When she went to the market with Dinah, she listened to the merchants discussing politics. Often, Dinah had to drag her away, scolding her for involving herself in matters for which she had no need. Sometimes she would sneak into the formal room to hear her father's discussion with his friends about Jewish law and practice. She discovered if she did not ask questions or make any sound, they appeared not to notice her. Rahel closed her eyes and went to sleep wondering what life as an exile would be like. She imagined herself as a grown woman able to see the world, not hidden inside her home and only visiting the hammam and her extended family under supervision.

Word traveled quickly through the Spanish community that Miguel Vide was working for the Romaniote Hayyim bar David. They waited to see how he would be treated. When they heard that Miguel was paid on Thursday evening so that his aunt would have money on Friday to prepare for the Sabbath, the community was satisfied. Hayyim was more than fair. No one else was paid with such consideration.

On Thursday evening, after their meager dinner, Clara washed the dishes and pots in the courtyard by the well with other women while Maria sat in their room and examined the sum in her lap.

Chapter 5

She had another almost equal amount arriving tomorrow from José. Slowly, the tears ran down her face.

"Daughter, what is it that makes you cry so?" asked Señora Vide gently.

"Look at this sum, Mother. When I was little, this was my allowance for sweets. My parents thought nothing of this sum of money. When I first married your son we would give three times this as a Christmas gift to the lowest servant in our house. Now, I am overwhelmed to have this same amount to feed my family of five," replied Maria almost weeping.

Señora Vide put her hand on her daughter-in-law's shoulder. She was at once overwhelmed by their good fortune, and saddened by how far they had fallen.

"Be careful," she warned, "to save a few pennies. There will be special foods to buy for Passover, when we celebrate the story of the Exodus. And with this extra money, we must put something away for Clara's dowry. She is getting old."

"Old! What do these people know?" retorted Maria, her tears now dry. "To marry a girl off by 14? She is barely old enough to take care of herself. Clara will not marry until 16."

"With our fortune," Señora Vide replied dryly, "she may not be able to marry at all." Then, with the money, they planned a small Sabbath feast to celebrate their good luck.

Early Friday morning Maria and Clara went to the shops. For the first time in their new home, they purchased candles. As Clara gently placed them into her bag, she commented, "How exquisite! Real candles. They will truly make our Sabbath special. Now, oil lamps are for the regular week only." Next they bought chickpeas, onions, spinach, fish, eggs, lemons, wine, and bread.

As their bags filled, Maria became more excited.

"Niece, now I will show you some recipes I learned in my parents' home as a child. Tonight will be special." While the two spent the day preparing the meal, Teresa cleaned and decorated. She smiled as she listened to her granddaughter and daughter-in-law cook together. Clara asked about Maria's childhood and soon Teresa was lost in another world—the world of courtiers and artists. She could hear the swish of ladies' dresses in the hallways, the sound of the music played by her mother on clavichord and by her sisters on viol and lute. They would play in the evenings, to the clink of silver and glass on the dining table as the maid set it for another elegant dinner party.

By the time the three women finished their work, their home had been transformed. The usually simple room had been turned into an elegant home. Teresa surveyed the room. "This is lovely. I do not think even the tables I set at home were more elegant." Maria gave a sad sigh, thinking of all the wonderful things they had had to leave behind.

Clara's face grew dark. "This is home. Home is where you are wanted. Spain we were expelled from." Then she too smiled as she looked around the room.

When Miguel and José returned Friday evening from the synagogue, they were greeted by an amazing sight. The room was usually spotless, but this evening, a new treat, with the glow of candles on the table, the house seemed mystical. Everything in the room danced as the flames flickered, making the plain objects pleasant to look at. And the aromas were overwhelming! A pot of chickpea and spinach soup bubbled over the cook stove and fish in an egg-and-lemon sauce waited on the side. The boys' mouths immediately began to water. They could not remember the last time they had eaten a meal so vast in flavor. Reverently, the blessings over the wine and bread were recited and then the family had a boisterous time celebrating their growing fortunes.

Chapter 6

Miguel arrived at work early every morning, and stayed late. He made himself useful in many ways. His hands were never idle. He swept the small store and the space in front of it whenever he had little else to do, or folded fabrics to keep them neat. By learning customers' preferences, Miguel often had the merchandise off the shelf before Hayyim or Mordechai could call for it.

He quickly learned his way around the many Jewish and non-Jewish neighborhoods. Before long, Miguel knew all of Thessaloniki and who lived where. Hayyim's customers soon began to seek him out for directions, or to deliver messages.

Miguel's presence in the store allowed Hayyim to make more visits to Muslim women forbidden to leave their homes in order to take their orders. This arrangement gave Mordechai more responsibility in the store. It also left Miguel and David together much of the time. David taught Miguel Greek and all about the fabrics, including how to identify by touch if they were wool, linen, or cotton. Miguel taught David Spanish and about the ports he had visited. He provided tales about the strange dress of the people of these places and divulged the few words he had collected along the way.

One day, as Miguel was gathering loose rolls of fabric to restack, Juan Abravanel appeared at the store. Miguel's neighbor walked into the store uncertainly, his eyes darting around the room. Their eyes met and Miguel strode across the room to greet his neighbor and friend.

"Señor Abravanel, what brings you to this illustrious establishment?" asked Miguel in Ladino.

"My boy," began Juan in the same language, "I would like to speak to your employer about a business opportunity. However," and here he paused, "you will have to speak for me. I cannot wrap my tongue around his strange language."

Miguel smiled, "Of course, I shall. Let me get Señor Hayyim." With that Miguel strode off to where Hayyim was selling some wool to an Ashkenazic customer.

"I believe this will work well for you," Hayyim commented to end the transaction.

"Oh yes!" was the excited response. "I remember the cold winters from my youth. This soft wool will make a lovely gift."

Hayyim saw Miguel waiting for him and signaled for him to wait a moment. Miguel looked at Juan across the room. Juan had turned his back to the room to study the fabrics. Miguel waited.

Finally, Hayyim turned to him, "Now what is it that makes you so anxious?"

"Kyrio Hayyim," began Miguel, "a friend is here to discuss business with you. His name is Juan Abravanel and his family and mine have shared our travels."

Hayyim smiled. The strange courtesies that the Spanish traded seemed peculiar, but he knew that men who traveled together had a special bond. Whatever the business, he was happy to listen because Miguel was extremely eager and helpful.

"Bring your friend and we will see what business he has," directed Hayyim. Miguel dutifully did as he was told and fetched Juan. Juan cleared his throat and looked expectantly at him. At first Miguel didn't get his meaning, but then he understood.

With a slight bow, he began, "Kyrio Hayyim, my friend Kyrio Abravanel would like to discuss a business proposition with you. He has asked me to be his," (and here Miguel paused as he did not know the word for "translator" — "voice" was the word he chose), "as he knows little Greek." The truth was he knew none, but Miguel didn't think the whole truth was necessary.

Juan began, "Señor Hayyim, at home in Spain I ran a large business doing what you do—selling fabrics. However, I employed the weavers myself. I had begun as a weaver and I wanted to make sure to provide the best product." Here he stopped and waited for Miguel to translate. Miguel took a breath to give himself time to figure out the best way to translate the meaning. Some of what Juan had said really should not be translated. Would Kyrio Hayyim respect Juan as much if he knew Juan had been a simple weaver?

"Kyrio Hayyim, in Spain I sold fabrics just as you do. This included working with the weavers." Miguel nodded to Juan to continue. Juan was a bit surprised at the brevity of the translation, but trusted his friend and so continued.

"I am returning to weaving and would like to know if you would be willing to buy my fabrics. A man of such importance should only have the best in his store."

Miguel took another breath. "I have decided to return to the root of the trade and work as a weaver. Would a righteous and honored man like you be willing to buy my humble cloth to sell in his much respected store?"

Hayyim pondered this request. He had no doubt that Miguel had translated liberally. He also believed that Miguel was being honest. What should he do? Could he work with this Spaniard? What would his kahal think? Would this be good for business or bad?

He stroked his beard and finally answered, "Kyrio Abravanel, without seeing the fine work that you do I am unsure if it is suitable for the needs of my clients. Bring me a bolt and then I will decide."

Miguel now turned to Juan. "Señor Abravanel, first bring me a piece of your finest fabric and then I will decide if your work is something my customers will be interested in."

When Hayyim heard Miguel complete the translation, he nodded his head in dismissal to Juan and went to help a customer.

Juan thanked Miguel for his help by using one of his endless traditional sayings, "Where there is life, there is hope." He then left the store unsure if he had gained anything. Miguel returned to his job of refolding bolts of fabric. He put Juan out of his mind believing he had done all he could and everything would turn out fine.

Miguel never brought lunch or asked for time to go home, and always insisted he was not hungry. Once, David shared his lunch with Miguel. He did not refuse the offer and ate with gusto, commenting on the unusual foods. David and Mordechai found this rather amusing, since this meal was always what was left from the previous day's dinner. David discussed this conversation with his mother; he was concerned because he had never known a family that did not have a full larder.

"A boy your age not hungry?" chided Hadassah. "Impossible. All boys your age are busy growing and working. Do not his grandmother and aunt know he will be hungry?"

"I think he is proud, Manna," replied David. "They have only his money and his cousin's—who is also an assistant." It troubled David greatly that he had so much and his friend had so little. He knew Miguel was often hungry.

Miguel, however, never mentioned it. He was usually hungry, but rarely ate three meals a day. Miguel and David never discussed these things, partially out of pride and partially because words would not change the situation. His working, however, would.

Hadassah made sure after that to send extra food. Hayyim noticed the extra food, and simply told Miguel to join them as his wife had sent too much and it should not go to waste. He and Hadassah never spoke of the extra lunches. After all, it would be against Jewish law to shame Miguel by pointing out how little he had and how much they had. He never said anything about the extra deliveries Miguel was making outside of his time for the shop either.

Passover was only a week away and Hayyim's business slowed. Everyone had bought fabrics for their new Passover clothes in the weeks before. Miguel and David spent much of their time in the store teaching each other. They spent their time testing each other's language skills. David would speak in Spanish, and Miguel in Greek, each correcting the other. It became a challenge as to who could speak longer without making a mistake. Hayyim was letting Miguel go home early telling him that he would be required to stay late another time.

Miguel used this time to deliver messages and packages for his side business. With the holiday approaching, he was busy making deliveries. Women were sending Passover pots to their daughters. Grandmothers had new Passover clothes sent to their grandchildren. And invitations to seders were sent around the community. By the end of each day, Miguel was exhausted.

One evening, when Hayyim and his family were enjoying a quiet gathering in the courtyard, David decided to ask a question he had been pondering. As was usual during these cool spring evenings, Rebecca and Hadassah were embroidering Rebecca's trousseau. Rahel was playing with her dolls. Hayyim and Mordechai were playing a board game. David was fixing a toy that Mimi had broken. Mimi was running around the courtyard and Dinah could be heard limping around the house. Now was the time and David plunged in.

"Is it not true," he said, glancing furtively at his father, "that for seder we are to invite one poor family, or at least one poor person? Preferably a stranger, someone new in the community?"

"Yes, my son," responded Hayyim putting down his playing pieces, eager for a conversation. "And my family has always honored that tradition, as I hope my children and their children will."

"Do you have a problem with this tradition?" asked Mordechai, always suspicious even of his brother's actions.

"No," replied David carefully. He knew for his plan to work, he had to speak his words with caution. "I think it is an important tradition for many reasons: one, because we really must take care of the poor; two, because how else will a stranger become part of the community unless introduced by someone who lives here; three, because perhaps this stranger has something of importance to share with the community."

Mordechai interjected haughtily, "Every Jew no matter how poverty stricken is important to the community." Although only two years David's senior, he believed himself far more mature and educated.

David was pleased; this was easier than he had dreamed.

"We have not decided on a guest this year, Father." Hayyim nodded his agreement. He had begun a family tradition where he suggested a few names and let his wife and sons argue for the guest of their choice. "I would like to recommend a family."

"Marvelous," commented his father. His soon-to-be son-in-law, Jacob, and Jacob's mother were the only guests this year so far, and he wanted to impress them with his sense of tzedakah. "Tell us who."

"Miguel and his family," spat out David. He had been afraid he would not be able to get the words out, but once they were, it seemed like a relief. He looked around at his family hoping their reaction would be positive, but certain that it would not be. He knew far too well what Mordechai's feelings were about Miguel, and all the Sephardim, as he was clear to tell anyone who entered the store. David was counting on his father's good nature to support his suggestion.

Everyone else stopped what he or she was doing. Mordechai dropped his playing pieces; the clatter echoed in the courtyard. He thought it was bad enough that Miguel had infiltrated their shop with his foreign words and ways. It was horrifying how quickly he had learned the business. It was almost terrifying the positive ways the customers responded to this upstart, but to have the help join them at a meal was unthinkable. Their usual guests were a visiting merchant or scholar, both respectable even if poverty stricken.

Rahel looked up, her eyes sparkling at the thought of someone new and interesting in the house. She had heard much about David's new Spanish friend, but since his first visit to request a job, she had not seen him.

Rebecca pricked her finger at the mention of the Vides. Her future husband was coming to seder. Why did David have to ruin that experience with those poor foreigners? If something happened, Jacob might reject her. Who would want her then? Once a suitor rejected a prospective bride, the whole community would consider her a suspect catch and her opportunities for a marriage within her circle would plummet. She might have to marry an uneducated man, or a sailor. She hung her head over her embroidery, sucking her finger.

Hayyim spoke first, "I'm not sure they are such a good choice. After all Miguel is an employee."

"Dinah shares our seder," David pointed out.

"But Dinah is a member of the family," explained Mordechai.

"No," corrected David, "she is a servant, really a slave, who we treat as a member of the family. Father paid her father the equivalent of a dowry for her to stay with us. No one else would take a poor hunchback girl with a limp into his home. Her father needed the money for his other daughters' dowries."

"They are ... Spanish," said Mordechai, almost whispering the last word as if it were a curse.

"They are Jews and poor, and Miguel is my friend," shouted David in their defense.

"Are they really Jews?" Hadassah asked in a half whisper, almost afraid to raise her voice and ask such a question. Everyone turned to look at her. This was the question they all wondered, but no one asked. "Are they changing their dishes, David? Do they keep kosher?"

David looked at his mother horrified. He was so angry he began to stutter, "B-b-but you send him food for lunch."

"I cannot bear to see anyone hungry when we have so much. It is rude for you three to eat and him not to." Hayyim smiled at his wife. Her generosity was one of the things he admired about her.

David was silenced for a moment, but only a moment.

"We have friends who belong to the Provençal synagogue," he said hopefully.

"They are different," retorted Mordechai. "They've been in Thessaloniki for a long time."

"All the better then. We are to invite strangers. Miguel's family has been here barely a year," David said triumphantly. "And," he added turning to his mother, "they must be Jews, the sultan said they were. The

Ashkenazim put their Torah in jackets and we put ours in a tik, but we accept them as Jews." With that David sat back triumphantly. He felt relieved that he had said all he had planned to and that it had been relatively well received. The rest of the family was quiet. Mimi got bored and started using his father's and brother's playing pieces as soldiers. The only sounds in the courtyard were Mimi's soldiers clacking on the stones and Dinah getting the evening fruit ready in the kitchen. As the silence continued, the air felt heavier. No one dared move.

Finally, Hayyim cleared his throat, "Hadassah, there will be five more for seder. Our guests will include Kyrio Miguel Vide and his family." He could see no good argument for David's answers. He tried hard not to pre-judge people and here was an opportunity to attempt some kind of relationship with the newcomers. Maybe they were not as terrible as other men in the community said they were.

Hadassah nodded her ascent. Rebecca opened her mouth and took a breath. She had to protest. She turned to her mother, unable to speak, with a pleading desperate look in her eyes. Her mother gave her a sharp glance and Rebecca returned to her sewing, her eyes overflowing with tears. This seder was to be proof to her future husband and mother-in-law of her capability and her family's standing in the community. While she knew little of politics and the differences among the Jewish communities, she had heard enough to frighten her. What if Jacob disapproved of their guests? The marriage would be canceled, the whole town would know why, and no man, no matter how poor, would marry her. Her life would end and she would become a burden to her father and then to Mordechai. The only person lower than her in the family hierarchy would be Dinah. She could never bear that.

Mordechai could not remember being angrier. His father had made a decision without a family discussion. Didn't his father realize how badly he had wanted to speak up? Why hadn't he specifically asked each person his or her feelings? How could he allow these people into their home? These people with divided loyalties: Christian and Jew. These people who tried to impose their unknowledgeable ways upon the Jewish community. He stood up so fast that his stool fell over.

"How ... but ... why don't you invite that weaver along as well?" and with that he huffed out of the courtyard to the echo of the fallen stool.

Rahel's eyes sparkled and she turned her bright smiling face to David. He had succeeded. Finally, something unusual was going to happen in their home. She would finally get to meet these strange new people. David winked at his little sister. He had succeeded! Miguel would come to his home as a guest.

"David," announced his father. "Since the choice was your suggestion, you have the honor of inviting them tomorrow after prayers."

David could barely contain his excitement.

"Yes, father," he said, his voice almost a whisper and his eyes glowing with anticipation.

Chapter

7

The next morning, when breakfast was finished, Hayyim bestowed his morning blessings: "My wife, may your day be filled with sunshine. Kooklia listen carefully to your mother, she is filled with wisdom. Rachamim, you little rascal, behave!" He paused and smiled at these people whom he loved so dearly and said, "Come my sons. It is time to find the perfect homes for our precious guests." David smiled a crooked smile—his father often spoke of the stock of fabrics that way. As the three men began their way out of the house, Hayyim turned to his younger son and said, "Remember, you may not say anything to Miguel until after evening prayers." And so the three began their day.

All day, David desperately wanted to tell Miguel the news.

He almost blurted out, "Miguel, you're all invited to our house for seder." But he had promised his father to wait until after evening prayers. Moreover, an invitation such as this must be made to the head of the family.

After they locked the store, David wished they would run to the synagogue. However, his father maintained his usual pace, greeting friends along the way. Then he wished they could hurry through prayers, but the rabbi and congregation spent the usual amount of time speaking with God. As soon as the closing prayer was said, David dashed out the door, almost knocking over the people around him, and sped through the streets. Through the neighborhoods he hurried until he came to the Vide house.

This was a poorer section of the town and David rarely came here. Those customers they had from here could not afford the fee of someone to carry the goods home. Occasionally, Hayyim sent David here to deliver some special order to an elderly lady who could not get to the store. However, since the Sephardim had taken over this neighborhood, the Romaniote had abandoned it, preferring to live with their own; thus, his opportunities to come here had decreased significantly in the last two years. Although the architecture throughout the city was similar, as he looked around he realized this neighborhood seemed different. Slowly, it occurred to David—here the houses seemed older; they were more worn and less cared for. After a few inquiries, David found the Vides' doorway. The smells in this area were different from those he knew. Someone was frying fish, but it smelled vinegary. A group of boys walked by carrying trays of borekia that gave off the most delicious aroma. He knocked on the door and, after a few moments, he heard some shuffling feet and then the door opened. A tall, stately woman stood there, dressed in clothes that were not only terribly worn, but also obviously foreign.

She looked at David in surprise and then spoke to him in accented Arabic, the common language of commerce. "What is it that you want?" she demanded. She did not know who this young man was, but knew him not to be Sephardic.

David was taken aback. The look of this woman was frightening. He had never seen anyone up close with a body shape like hers, tight in the middle from a corset and with starched skirts on the bottom. And she asked him questions without inviting him in. His mother always invited guests in without a word, and immediately sought out his father or Mordechai.

However, he quickly recovered from the social faux pas and responded, "My name is David bar Hayyim and I am seeking Kyrio Vide."

"Ah" she said, her face softening. "Miguel's employer. Please, come in. My grandsons have not yet returned from evening prayers. Let me offer you a glass of wine while you wait." She stood back from the door to let him in, just as she would have done at her home in Spain. David stepped across the threshold, and into another world. Señora Vide had done the best she could to re-create her former home. The ledge under the window was covered in cushions for a seat, and the others around the room were used as beds with a blanket rolled on the end. In the middle of the room were five rickety stools and a table. On a shelf were a stack of plates and bowls and two candlesticks. There were no decorations on the walls, but in one corner was a dark chest and in another a small cook stove. David took a seat on one of the stools and took the glass of cheap wine that was offered. The seat was uncomfortable and foreign and the silence unnerving, but each waited, Señora Vide at the stove, stirring a large pot, and David alone at the simple table.

Two pairs of feet were heard outside. Relieved, David turned toward the door in anticipation. It flung open and two veiled women came in. They did not notice David in the semidarkness of the room.

Maria threw off her peçe in a most ungraceful manner, "I hate these things. They make life outside most cumbersome."

"But Tía," came a much younger muffled voice as she folded her own and her aunt's, "they are terribly beautiful." Clara turned around and her large hazel eyes alighted on David. They sparkled with interest. This stranger was obviously wealthy. She touched her aunt, and nodded her head in David's direction.

Señora Vide introduced them using Arabic, "David bar Hayyim, this is my daughter-in-law Maria Vide and my granddaughter Clara Vide." Suddenly, Clara felt shy. Around other Marranos she knew how to act, but this was a Romaniote. How was she to address this person? Was it even appropriate to address him? She had never had personal contact with one. Her life was centered on her neighborhood and her family. Other than going to the markets, she did not leave her enclave.

David did not know how to respond. He had never been introduced to a woman before unless she came into the shop for cloth, but that was business and they were veiled and always chaperoned. So he nodded to each. He felt even more uncomfortable being alone in a room with three women than he had with one. If his friend did not arrive very soon, David decided, he would have to leave and wait outside. Luckily, at that moment Miguel and José opened the door.

They each hugged Maria and Teresa with much affection before Clara could whisper, "Miguel, Señor David is here."

Miguel turned to David with a mixture of embarrassment and excitement. As much as he wanted David to meet his family, he also knew how foreign the experience was for him. Miguel was embarrassed by the homemade furniture that he knew David had never seen before. In addition, it had taken him a while to become accustomed to the way in which David and his father and brother reacted to each other. Miguel knew that David's affection for his mother and sisters was just as strong as his for his sister, aunt, and grandmother, but David almost never spoke about them and certainly never touched them in public. Miguel struggled every day not to mention some advice his grandmother or aunt had given him. It was very difficult for him not to hold his sister's hand as they walked on the pier or through the market. This new world of separateness was so hard to understand.

José quickly realized his role as patriarch and sat down next to David and asked in stilted Greek, "Señor David, to what do we owe the honor of your company in our humble house? I hope it is good news."

David turned to him gratefully and put his glass of wine on the table. He could focus on José and try not to think about the strange forthright women in the room, or how his friend had greeted his aunt and sister—it seemed so childish.

"Kyrio Vide, my father would like the honor of your family's company at our seder next week," he said gravely in his thickly accented Spanish.

José first turned to his grandmother and mother for advice. They tried to remain neutral, knowing that it would be inappropriate in this new country for them to speak, at least in front of male guests. José realized his error in turning to them when his mother simply raised her shoulders in a questioning manner and switched his gaze to Miguel, who raised his eyebrows to say yes.

José cleared his throat and said in his most formal though heavily accented Greek, "We are … pleased to be … the guests of such … an important man. I doubt our presence would be … half the honor as the invitation. This is an important … matter and I will have an answer for you … on the next day." Then he added in a personal tone, "You must stay and have supper with us." Señora Vide smiled graciously hiding the fact that she hoped he would not stay; there was barely enough for them.

David courteously declined and left the Vide home, hurrying home to eat his supper. The thought of staying and eating with the Vides was terrifying. What did they eat? How did they eat it? Especially since Kyria Vide dressed so frighteningly.

Once the door shut behind him, the four Vides sat down as one. They stared at each other in disbelief.

José began in their native Ladino, "I'm not sure I did the right thing. Was it insulting not to give an answer immediately?"

"Señor Hayyim is making quite a statement by inviting us," remarked the matriarch, as much to herself as to those around the table. "By accepting the invitation, we will be guests of an important member of the Romaniote community. This dinner could help us gain acceptance to the larger Jewish community. But I do find their superstitious Jewish practices hard to swallow. What if they discover how little we know of the customs?"

Miguel hung his head, discouraged. He had made a good friend and learned about the local customs of his adopted community. Now his grandmother was going to make him insult his friend and employer by rejecting the invitation.

Clara saw the look on her brother's face. She desperately wanted him to be happy.

"His Spanish is amazing, Miguel. You are a good teacher," she commented with honest enthusiasm. General agreement passed around the table and then silence settled again.

José was torn.

He spoke out loud, as much to himself as to those around him, "What a wonderful opportunity. David's family, they are generous, kind people. A good meal is tempting. But they are rather wealthy, not what we had been though … and now …." José looked around the room sadly.

He was worried not only about not understanding the local customs and traditions, but also about the fact that they were poor. How could they present themselves appropriately at a rich man's house; they did not have the right clothes.

Clara kept silent because she had little to say. She had never received an invitation to dine somewhere else; in fact, she had never eaten any place but her aunt's table. The idea was exciting; the prospect of seeing Señor David again appealing. He was handsome and articulate. Then she too realized that she had nothing to wear. Her clothes were a hodge-podge of pieces she had bought and bartered from the marketplace to replace the old Spanish clothes she had outgrown. This mishmash was certainly not appropriate for a special occasion at a grand house.

"Ai, the soup!" yelped Maria. She grabbed the spoon and stirred furiously. Then she moved the pot off the fire and served everyone a bowl of what they called soup. In reality, it was little more than gruel. They ate in continued silence.

"Come," said José when they had finished, "we must make a decision. I believe we should go. We have traveled the world and seen sights most people never do. What can they do that we cannot match? And who is to judge a man by his clothes. We should show them it is not the clothing that makes the man, but education, compassion, and understanding." Miguel's sullen look broke like the sun emerging from behind a storm cloud. Clara's mind spun. An invitation to a real Romaniote house! Now she would know what their houses look like. What they wear. Even what they eat. She was almost too excited to sit still. Teresa and Maria looked at each other in amazement. José had never asserted himself before. When had he suddenly matured?

Chapter
8

In the Spanish neighborhood, news of the invitation spread quickly. Some were horrified that the Vide family would be guests of a Romaniote family—people who sneered at the immigrants. Others viewed this as a step for the entire Spanish community to become integrated into the local Jewish community. Still others did not understand the fuss; the Romaniote community was terribly small compared to theirs—such politics seemed inconsequential. Really, these last people felt, the only people to be concerned about were the Muslims since they were the ones in power.

Hayyim's family knew nothing about the scandal they and the Vides were involved in among the Sephardim. In reality, Hayyim and his sons were relatively untouched by anything to do with Passover. The women, however, were consumed with the holiday. Hadassah was busy cleaning her house. She and Dinah scrubbed everything. Rebecca watched enthusiastically, making mental notes of what they were cleaning with what brushes, rags, and supplies.

"Stop watching and start working," nagged her mother. "You do not learn by watching; you learn by doing. Go into the sealed barrels in the corner of the kitchen. On the top of one should be a cloth. Cover the long table with it and then stack all the Passover meat dishes on the table. Let me know if any are broken."

"Of course, Manna," came Rebecca's reply. Soon, she realized she would be doing this exchange of everyday and Passover dishes in her own home next year. Her own home, she thought to herself—a home where she would direct the servants. A home where she would decorate the rooms and have her children and watch them grow. The excitement wore off quickly, however. Bending into the barrels was back breaking work and Mimi was running around her feet trying to get into the barrels.

"Rahel, Rahel! Take Mimi away. I will trip and break Manna's dishes," shouted Rebecca.

"Coming, coming," yelled Rahel, but not soon enough. A crash, curses, and then crying were heard and Rahel, Hadassah, and Dinah ran out of the house and across the courtyard to the kitchen. There was Rebecca, tears streaming down her face, chasing Mimi. Mimi was running around the table in the kitchen laughing and holding a large piece of what had been a serving tray. Rahel ran into the fray and captured Rachamim. Then the two shame-faced girls turned to their mother. Scattered on the floor were pieces of the tray.

At first glance the scene was funny and Hadassah laughed, until she saw the shards of the tray on the floor and then stopped immediately.

"What is this mess?" she demanded.

"Manna, I'm sorry, truly I am. I was doing as you said. I took the dishes from the barrel to the table. But Mimi was pulling on my entari and as I turned I hit the platter on the table," sobbed Rebecca. She was sure her mother would never forgive her for breaking a dish.

Hadassah looked sternly at Rahel. Rahel looked to the floor trying to hold Rachamim still in her arms. Rahel knew that no matter what Rachamim did, it was her fault. Her job was to make sure he did not get into any trouble. Besides he was the family pet, and really could not do anything wrong.

"Rahel, take Mimi into the courtyard to play. Rebecca clean up the mess. Dinah, we need to finish." She turned haughtily and left the room. Dinah silently, as was her custom, followed her mistress. Rahel scuttled after them dragging a sullen Mimi by one arm. Rebecca's sobs turned into hiccups as she collected the pieces of the platter. Hadassah was not concerned about the dish. There were plenty more, but she did not want her daughters to take the matter lightly. She would speak to them later.

Life was very different in Señora Vide's house. The three women examined the coins they had and made a shopping list.

Clara mentioned innocently, trying to be helpful, "I have heard in the market and among friends that one is supposed to change dishes for Passover."

Señora Vide snorted, "Yes. What a silly bunch of superstitious nonsense. One is also supposed to have separate dishes for milk and meat. We wash our dishes, what more should we do? Besides, we've barely money enough as it is. How could we afford more dishes if there is barely enough for food? This year, we will not have to beg for matzah, thankfully, and can celebrate openly. Let us be happy with that." That ended that conversation.

The days leading to the seder were equally stressful for both families. Clara could barely contain her excitement. Every day brought an adventure in preparation.

"Abuela, tell me again the meaning of Passover." "Abuela, what foods will we eat?" "Abuela, what is a seder?" In the middle of the week Clara and Maria took out the good outfits for each member of the family. Once they had made the decision to go to the seder, Maria and Teresa had decided to buy the younger people new clothes, or relatively new clothes. Maria had gone to the market and made the purchases; there was even enough to buy herself a newer outfit with some hard bargaining. They spent the day brushing, washing, and mending. Clara was ecstatic! She tried on her new clothes. "Oh how wonderful these are!" she exclaimed. "Tía, I believe we tie the waist of the salvar and then these ribbons on the ankles." Maria chuckled as she looked at the young woman, naked except for a pair of baggy men's trousers. "Then I put on the kamiza. Look at these elegant sleeves. Abuela, look at the embroidery at the end of the sleeves, here at my elbow, and at the bottom. See how my salvar shows under the entari, it should never reach to the ground. That is what the woman said who sold it to me." Teresa smiled indulgently at the joy in her granddaughter's voice and on her face. "Oh Abuela you should try these clothes. It is so free. No corset to make me stand so straight and keep my breath so tiny. I can bend any way I wish!"

When Clara began her work on Teresa's clothes, she could not contain herself any longer, "Abuela, when are you going to get some new clothes? This dress and ruff are so … so Spanish. We are not in Spain; we are not wanted in Spain. Please, let us go buy you a entari and salvar."

"Clara," hissed her aunt, "that is rude!"

Teresa looked up from the cooking pot.

"Clara, my child, these are the types of clothes I have always worn. Even if the King does not consider me a Spaniard, I feel as one. Our family had been there for many generations. They are who I am."

"But Abuela," whined Clara. "We've been invited to dinner. And not just any dinner, but seder. And not just any place, but an important family and Miguel's employer. We need to make a good impression."

"Clara," reprimanded her aunt, "A proper lady does not speak to her elders that way. Apologize!"

"I am sorry, Abuela," said Clara, tears in her eyes for being reprimanded. Very quietly and sincerely almost into the outfit in her lap, she added in a barely audible whisper, "But you need some new clothes."

Teresa walked to Clara's chair and stood behind her resting her hands on her granddaughter's shoulders, "Someday you may understand this, but it is hard for an old woman to change her ways." However, Señora Vide, daughter of a wealthy Marrano pawnbroker, did something she would never have done before; she went to a neighbor and borrowed clothes. Despite what she said to her granddaughter, Teresa did remember her own youth and the desire to be fashionable. She understood Clara's wish to look like everyone else. Additionally, though Teresa did not like to state this out loud, she knew that returning to Spain was impossible for not only her family, but the entire community. Thus, for her grandchildren she had to make an effort to be part of this Ottoman community. This was their home now.

In the Romaniote neighborhood, Hadassah and the ever-silent Dinah were busy gathering all the special ingredients for this extra special seder. She must impress Jacob and his mother for Rebecca's sake. As much as they would be judging Rebecca, they would also be judging her. The daughter was a reflection of the mother. So Hadassah was making doubly sure everything was perfect. The extra five people were troubling. Not that she ever objected to more people. Tzedakah was her pride. What concerned her was who these five were. What did the neighbors think? And their families, what would they think? What would Kyrio Jacob think? Despite her reassurances to her daughter, she had had many long discussions with her husband in the privacy of their bed about his choice of guests.

"Are you sure, husband, that this is a wise choice?" she had asked that first night when he had made his pronouncement.

"I cannot argue with David's reasoning. It is the same that I have given to the children," was his careful reply.

"But these are not visitors to the town. These are not rabbis traveling to the Holy Land, or merchants stopping to trade; these are people who are staying," she argued.

"Yes, and so they need to be introduced to the community. They need to be accepted," he tried to reason. "The sultan believes these people will help Thessaloniki and that they are Jews. Maybe, if we invite them in, we can teach them how to be proper Jews." Hadassah was not convinced.

"I am not a teacher," she warned her husband. "I am a mother and a wife. My duty is to you and our children. I do not like this idea because I do not want Rebecca's chance at marriage to be jeopardized." The conversation ended there and continued many nights with the same words. She knew that the invitation could not be undone and Hayyim knew that she needed to voice her concerns.

As she neared her house, her thoughts focused on the immediate problems she could deal with, like tonight would be the last night they would have bread with their dinner. Tomorrow would be the final cleaning of hametz, leavening, from the house and then they would be ready for seder the following night.

In the meantime, Rebecca was putting the final stitches on their new clothes. At least that was what she was supposed to be doing. Mostly, she was admiring her new outfit and dreaming of next year when she would organize a seder for Jacob, her husband.

Chapter
9

The next morning, Dinah prepared the family's breakfast. Hadassah made a practice of sleeping late the day of seder. She would be up extremely late serving the guests and cleaning up. Once the men left for the store and Dinah had fed Rebecca, Rahel, and Mimi and cleaned the kitchen, Hadassah rose and put on an old outfit.

She ate her breakfast and called Dinah and Rebecca into the kitchen. "It is time to begin preparing for seder. First we must prepare the lamb and then we will cook everything else."

While Rebecca had seen the lamb roasted numerous times before, this time she took careful note of the height of the flame in the spit and the spices her mother rubbed into the flesh. Next year, she hoped to make this at her new home. Rebecca knew that her mother's cooking was considered the best in the family and she planned on continuing that tradition. Dinah started gathering the dates, walnuts, honey, and wine for the haroset, and washing the rice. Slowly, as the day progressed the feast appeared in the kitchen. They prepared eggs boiled with red onionskins, leek croquettes, meat pies made with matzah, and rice with fava beans. For dessert, macaroons; Rebecca loved them, but grinding the almonds was exhausting work.

Just as Hayyim, David, Mordechai, and Miguel were about to leave, Juan Abravanel appeared with a bolt of fabric. Miguel saw him at the door and his face broke into a smile. He practically ran across the store to greet his friend.

"My friend Señor Vide, I have brought a sample for your employer," said Juan cheerfully.

"Come, come," replied Miguel. They both went to see Hayyim.

"Kyrio Hayyim," began Miguel, "my neighbor Kyrio Abravanel has come to sell you some fabric."

Hayyim sighed deeply. He didn't relish this conversation. The day upon which Passover began was a day he preferred not to conduct business, but to complete any unfinished work he could and give the store a good cleaning. Besides, many of his relatives and friends spoke against the newly arrived Spanish Jews. They thought them arrogant and lackadaisical in their religious practice. Some of his cousins, the finest merchants and scholars in Thessaloniki, had been accused of being backward and unsophisticated by the Sephardim. Hayyim was not convinced that doing business with a Sephardic Jew would be advantageous, nor was he sure it would harm his business either. He weighed his options quickly.

"Come, Kyrio Abravanel, show me your sample," he said in his most cordial tone, never letting on his internal conflict. This comment needed no translation. Juan bowed low and put his bolt of fabric on the table.

Both Mordechai and David came over to the table. David waited expectantly. He reached out and stroked the fabric. Mordechai was colder and raised a haughty eyebrow at Juan and Miguel. Hayyim felt the fabric between his thumb and forefinger, testing the weight and texture of the material. He stroked his beard.

"This is fine fabric, not quite what we are used to selling," Hayyim said slowly as he studied the material.

Miguel translated, "This cloth is good, but different from my usual." Juan breathed deeply. Hayyim looked up from the fabric and at Juan the weaver.

"This is what I shall do for a friend of our Miguel," smiled Hayyim. The fondness he had for Miguel was hard for him to hide and Miguel appreciated the language his employer used. "I will take this bolt and we will see how it sells." Juan saw the change in Hayyim's face and heard Miguel's name and felt his spirit rise as he turned to Miguel.

"For a friend of our Miguel," Miguel grinned as he spoke, "I will buy this bolt of fine fabric. If it sells, then I will purchase another."

Juan smiled and nodded graciously at Hayyim. Hayyim took his purse off his belt and took out some coins. Juan shook his head and held up his fingers. The bargaining had begun. Miguel realized he was not needed for this part of the conversation. Sometimes the common language of money and numbers did not need a translator. He winked at David. David winked back and they left the table. David smiled at Miguel.

"Your friend makes a fine fabric. It is not Italian wool cloth, but it is well woven," commented David.

"I am glad your father bought it. Juan really needs the money," responded Miguel. At that moment, Juan walked past the boys, slapped Miguel on the back, and left the shop obviously pleased.

Hayyim called out, "Miguel, we are done for the day. Go to the hammam, go home, get ready for seder." It was clear he was feeling particularly generous. Miguel bowed to his employer, grinned at his friend, and ran out of the door hoping to catch up with Juan. "David, Miguel forgot to sweep in front of the store, make sure it is extra clean in time for the holiday."

"Of course, Father," replied his son dutifully. After all, there was a holiday just upon them. So he took the broom and went outside.

Hayyim then turned to his son Mordechai. "I felt the ice in here every time you looked at Kyrio Abravanel. You must do something about this problem."

"But Father," protested Mordechai, "you know how those people feel about us. How can you buy from him?"

"Firstly," responded his father sternly, "I know how some of the Sephardim feel about us, the Romaniote, but I certainly do not know how this man feels about either my people or me. Secondly, the only way that we will learn to work with the Sephardim is to actually work with the Sephardim and so I have. Thirdly, you need to examine the man. It was clear to me he is much in need and this simple transaction will afford him the opportunity to celebrate the holiday. If nothing else, view my action as tzedakah."

Mordechai looked at his father without comprehension. "Father, you cannot change people. They will always be different."

"Exactly," was his father's strong response. "They will always be different, just as the Ashkenazim, Ottomans, or Christians are. But every person deserves tzedakah if he or she needs it. Now," and he gave Mordechai a dark look, daring him to speak again, "take this bolt and put it on the bottom of the pile in that far corner."

"But," protested Mordechai, "that will place it in the darkest corner. No one will see it. No one will buy it. You will have wasted your money."

"It is an act of tzedakah. And who said no one will buy it?" was the curt reply. Thus, the conversation ended.

Late in the afternoon when the meal was almost done, Hayyim, David, and Mordechai appeared. They had closed the shop early so that they could go to the hammam before the holiday began and be home in time to let the women and children go as well. Hadassah checked her various pots and gathered the household around her for their trip to the hammam. She and Rebecca led the procession, followed by Rahel and Mimi, and finally Dinah with a parcel of towels and clean clothes. This small group joined numerous other cliques of women exiting and entering their homes on their way to or from the baths.

As the little group passed each family, they wished them a good holiday and asked about the men folk and the women who were not with them. This was a rare time in the Jewish quarter of Thessaloniki when the streets were filled with women and children and men were scarce. Women took advantage of this opportunity and strolled through the neighborhoods gossiping with their friends and relations. Hadassah was no exception. With the children around her and Dinah to mind them, she enjoyed this chance to visit with friends of her childhood whom she rarely saw because they too were busy with their homes and families and rarely allowed to leave their houses. Thus, the way to the hammam was not only crowded, but also slow moving.

At the hammam, Hadassah gave a small sum to the attendant so that she would watch their things and keep them dry. Then Hadassah took Rebecca around to see where the married women chatted. Dinah took Rahel and Mimi to the baths directly, washed them, dressed them, and sent them to the courtyard to play with the other children. Then she joined Hadassah and Rebecca. Although she was neither married nor engaged, because of her age (around 30) she was allowed to join in with this group. Everyone in town knew she would never marry; a servant with a humpback and limp had no chance of finding a husband, so they treated her with sympathetic kindness. Besides, she considered it her duty to make sure that Hadassah and Rebecca were taken care of, even here in the baths.

Rebecca was being overwhelmed by the advice and stories the other women were giving her. She sat in her robe with her eyes wide, absorbing everything that was said to her. The women around her gave her advice on how to please her mother-in-law: never argue with her; accept her advice with a smile; compliment her clothes, cooking, or decorating. Some told great fictions about how their mother-in-laws mistreated them, or checked their sheets for signs that a baby might be on the way. However, a few tried to impart some real advice like how to manage a home with a mother-in-law in residence, or how to get the servants to work with her rather than to side with the mother-in-law. Hadassah sat next to her tittering, many of the stories being told were to frighten or shock the soon-to-be bride. She had done just that herself to other soon-to-be brides. Dinah sat near them and listened, her eyes gleaming with laughter.

Once it was their turn at the baths, the three women washed themselves, dried, dressed, and gathered Rahel and Mimi. They wished the attendant a good holiday and hurried home to finish the preparations. Along the way, they wished their friends and relatives a good holiday. However, they did not stop to gossip or meander down the streets. Hadassah knew that it was late and there was much work to be done in the house before seder. None of the other women returning home stopped either. The time for fun was over and the housework had to be done before the holiday began.

When the family returned, Hadassah, Rebecca, and Rahel turned the formal room into a place of wonder. They gave Mimi the job of fluffing the cushions. Dinah stayed in the kitchen watching the food. Couches were placed around the low table for the men and cushions on the benches against the walls for the women. The best carpets were rolled out on the floor and one was placed on the table in the center of the room. The silver Rahel had not so patiently polished earlier in the day appeared on the table.

"There now," commented Hadassah with a deep sigh of contentment, "that does look good."

Rahel examined the room.

"Oh yes, Manna! Look at how the silver shines," she said contentedly. Her hard work really did change the room. The Kiddush cup shone as if with a light of its own. Hadassah kissed her gently on the top of head.

Rebecca surveyed the room, "Yes, mother. Lovely. Kyrio Jacob will like it. I hope." She added the last statement with some hesitation. What if he did not like the room? Would he hold that against her and say that she will not make a good housewife?

"Who cares what Kyrio Jacob believes," was Rahel's curt reply. "I like it. Do you Mimi?" When she got no response, she turned around and realized that Rachamim had snuck out of the room. "Mimi! Mimi, where are you?" she called out crossly as she ran out into the courtyard. "Mimi, you better not get yourself dirty!"

Rebecca turned to her mother unsure of what to think and saw the sparkle in her mother's eyes. They both broke out in loud laughter. They knew, just as Rahel did, that Rachamim was going to be dirty. Hadassah knew she would normally be quite angry with her two youngest, but not today, not now. She was tired. A whole week of work had gone into today. Hadassah looked at Rebecca. It was good to see her eldest laugh. So they laughed until the laughter was done. Then they dried their tears and arm in arm left the formal room to see what damage

Mimi had done to himself and Rahel, and how Dinah was doing with the food.

They found Rahel and Rachamim in the courtyard. It was obvious that he had, yet again, been digging in one of the flowerpots. His arms were covered in dirt and there were smudges on his face.

Rahel sat exasperated on a bench watching him try to brush off his hands, "All the work Dinah spent in getting you clean. Wait until Moth…" and she broke off because there was their mother. She looked at her mother with pleading eyes hoping she would realize that Mimi was out of her control.

"Rachamim bar Hayyim," said Hadassah sternly. He cringed. He was only called that for very good or very bad reasons. He doubted that this was a good one. "You are a mess! We just went to the baths. Well, go to the kitchen and have Dinah wash you. Then go sit quietly in the kitchen. Do not touch anything, do not play with anything, and do not do anything until I get there. Is that clear?" Rachamim nodded quietly without looking at his mother. He gave one last brush of his hands in a vain attempt to remove the dirt and slunk off to the kitchen.

Now Rahel looked up with fear in her eyes. Rebecca felt sorry for her. If her mother had been that stern with Mimi, what lay in store for Rahel. Hadassah sat heavily on the bench beside Rahel and took the girl's hand in hers. "He is quite a handful, is he not, kookla. Well, it is good that he will be starting school shortly. Mimi is really getting too big for you to handle on your own." This was said so gently that Rahel and Rebecca looked at their mother in shock. "All my little ones are growing up," Hadassah continued without looking at anyone, only at Rahel's small smooth hand. "That is as it should be. You are all a fine bunch: respectful, smart, and healthy. What more could a mother want. It does not matter. Soon there will be grandchildren." At this, Rebecca blushed. "Come daughters," Hadassah sighed as much to herself as them, "it is time to finish the preparations." Then she released Rahel's hand and pushed herself up from the bench with effort, as if getting up required much work. However, once up she smoothed her clothes and returned to her normal confidence and jubilance.

Chapter
10

About an hour before sunset, Jacob bar Isaac and his mother arrived. Rebecca opened the door and silently showed them into the formal room. There Hayyim greeted his future in-laws and then Hadassah arrived and showed her daughter's future mother-in-law into the everyday room. Here the women could sit and chatter neither disturbing nor being disturbed by the men. Rebecca remembered her manners and slipped out to the kitchen to get some refreshments.

"Dinah, she's so old," commented Rebecca as she entered the kitchen.

"Who, my pet?" asked Dinah without looking up from the pot.

"Kyrio Jacob's mother, of course."

"Silly koritzi," laughed Dinah. "Of course she is old. She is older than your mother and Kyrio Jacob is nearer your father's age than Mordechai's." Rebecca sat down heavily on a stool. "Now what is the problem?" Dinah asked as she shuffled toward the girl.

"I had not thought about that. Why must I marry such an old man?" asked Rebecca, half to herself and half to Dinah.

"He is not that old—only around 40. And he is very important. With many sisters to marry off, he had to pay off all the debt from their dowries before he could find a wife. This is the age most men marry and most girls marry at yours. You are lucky," now Dinah sounded wistful, "to have not only a husband, but a middle class scholar as a husband. How can any girl complain about having such a husband? Or any husband and home of her own? Oh Rebecca," she cried, full of her own longing for a family that she would never have, "stop being foolish and take these trays back before you are missed!"

61

Dutifully, Rebecca took the two trays of pickled vegetables, one for the men and one for the women, and walked back. She thought about what Dinah said. It really had not occurred to her how old her husband would be. Her thoughts had been focused on her new position in society, a married woman versus a girl, not on her husband. Dinah was right of course; she was lucky to get such an important husband. Besides, her father was older than her mother, so were her uncles older than her aunts. She decided to go to her mother first, so that she would have more time studying Kyrio Jacob when she brought the second tray.

When Rebecca entered the everyday room, her mother and future mother-in-law were catching up on local gossip. Hadassah nodded in approval as Rebecca put the tray on the table. Just then Mimi burst in with Rahel in tow. The quiet room was suddenly filled with noise. Rebecca smiled to herself imagining her own children soon to come and exited the room quietly.

Hayyim, Jacob, Mordechai, and David made themselves comfortable on the cushions. Jacob began the conversation, "Hayyim, how is your experiment with the Spanish boy? You know, you have become the only topic of conversation in the community."

David's face contorted into a disgusted look. "Kyrio Jacob, Miguel is not an experiment. He is a person."

"David, show some respect to your elders," chided Hayyim. He turned to his future son-in-law. "Our new employee," and he pronounced these words carefully, "is fine. He is bright and eager. He has an accent, but then so do many others in the Jewish community. He has different customs, but we've accepted the Ashkenazim and their Torah mantles."

"I hope it works out well. You can never tell what those people will do," replied Jacob dismissively as he settled on a cushion.

David did not like this conversation at all. He thought quickly about a way to change it. "Kyrio Jacob, what interesting letters have you written to the sultan recently?"

Jacob, ever vain, was quite willing to step into that conversation. "As you know, few people in Thessaloniki can write Arabic as well as I can. I really should not discuss much of what I write, but the …."

Without even creaking the door, Rebecca entered the formal room, trying not to disturb the conversation. Slowly, she offered each a treat before she settled the tray on a corner table. Then she made as if to fix various cushions, so that she had an excuse to stay in the room and study her fiancé. As she watched him, he seemed to grow in stature. The gray in his beard stood out to her as did the wrinkles in his face. His voice was deep and to Rebecca, his words profound. His age dimmed in importance and his intellect grew. Rebecca imagined her position as the wife of an important scholar—how important she would be in the community. Her kitchen would be busy preparing delicacies for the many guests that would come to request favors of her husband. Her house would be filled with guests from all over.

Jacob droned on for quite a while. At least, pondered David, he is not being nasty about Miguel. Then David realized Jacob and his father were discussing the hot topic—the overwhelming number of Spaniards in the community.

"… How can we make the sultan understand? To him, and thus to all the Muslims including our own governor, all Jews are Jews. They do not understand that we are very different in our practices and customs. However, the most pressing problem is the population that is overwhelming our allotted space in the city," commented Hayyim.

"It is much more than that," interjected Jacob. "Already, the Jewish courts are overburdened with cases. Did you hear about the Spanish woman who took a Romaniote butcher to the courts for not selling her kosher meat? Poor lady made a fool of herself," chuckled Jacob. "The butcher was not only the nephew of one of the court rabbis, but all three of the rabbis had trained him in kashrut."

"What happened?" asked Mordechai.

Jacob responded, "She lost her case, of course."

"But worse than that," jumped in Hayyim "now the community is divided. The Spanish are starting their own butcheries and refusing to buy from ours. Rabbis are arguing over what really is kashrut and who has the right to verify that meat is kosher."

David was drawn into the conversation, "But how many ways are there to slaughter an animal?"

"My boy, that is not the point," replied Jacob. "The real argument is over who will control the community. A number of us are already discussing the preservation of our services."

"Preservation?" ask David shocked. "They have always been the same, what will change?" Rebecca stopped pretending to rearrange cushions. She pondered the discussion. It made little sense to her.

"How could there be another Jewish way of doing things? The rabbis read the laws and explained them. What other interpretation could there be? How could Judaism change? It had always been this way and these newcomers just have to accept this," were her thoughts as the men continued their discussion.

Jacob's chest swelled as he now could discuss his work. "This is not the first time recording our prayers has been discussed among scholars. In the past, we have not been that concerned, however. The Ashkenazic and Provençal communities are terribly small compared to our own. The numbers of the Sephardim are overwhelming. Their services are a mishmash of ideas and languages. We do not want their prayers mixed with our. If we write them, then we are assured this will not happen."

"Who will do this?" wondered Hayyim out loud.

"That is a serious question," responded Jacob.

Now Mordechai chimed in, "Why does not the court just dictate that only the Romaniote rituals are allowed."

"Mordechai!" reprimanded Hayyim. "Have you forgotten the Ashkenazic, Provençal, and Venetian communities?"

"No, Father," he responded. "But one set of practices, one group of rabbis, that would make everything easier."

Jacob turned to Mordechai. "In many ways you are right. However, they are guests of the sultan, just as we are. In fact, the sultan has decreed that any mistreatment of these refugees will result in punishment by his courts. So long as HE believes them to be Jews …"

David cleared his throat as loudly as he could without seeming too obvious. Rebecca had left the door open behind her when she had entered the room and so they had not heard the Vide family enter the room. Dinah must have let them in. Miguel and José knew enough Greek to understand the conversation they had interrupted, even though it was in Yevanic. The Vide women had learned the words "Spanish" and "Jew" in Greek and could tell by the tone of the voices that it was not a positive reference. Rebecca's heart sank. Her engagement was over, her future destroyed.

Hayyim was not pleased by the turn of events, but had to keep everyone peaceful. He naturally switched to Greek and introduced their latest arrivals, "Kyrio Jacob bar Isaac, these are Kyries Miguel and José Vide. Kyrio Miguel is our employee and a friend of David's." Rebecca nodded to Miguel and José and then silently ushered the women out of the room to the next one, where her mother and future mother-in-law were.

The women immediately stopped talking. Hadassah rose, "Welcome! I am Hayyim's wife Hadassah and this is Miriam, soon to be Rebecca's mother-in-law. These are my daughters: Rebecca and Rahel, and my youngest Rachamim."

There was a moment of silence. If Hadassah had not pointed to each person, Teresa and Maria would never have guessed her meaning. Their Greek was almost non-existent.

Clara took the initiative and spoke for her grandmother and aunt, "This is my ... grandmother Teresa Vide and my ... aunt Maria Vide, and I am Clara. They do not speak Greek and I am sorry ... for my bad Greek."

Hadassah motioned them to sit and said kindly to Clara, "You must speak for them in your beautiful Greek."

Clara and Rebecca eyed each other, realizing that they were the same age. Yet they seemed so different to each other. Clara could not imagine being married so young. Rebecca could not imagine traveling around the world, especially since she had never been out of Thessaloniki.

The room was quiet except for Mimi babbling to himself. Hadassah used this moment to look out the window at the sky.

"Come," she said, "the first star will appear any moment. It is time to begin." With Hadassah leading the way, the women and Mimi walked into the formal room.

Chapter
11

When the women and children entered the room as the first star appeared, the men fell silent. It would be inappropriate to speak politics or business in front of them. Besides, a holiday was about to start. Hadassah lit the festival candles and chanted the blessing, a daughter on each side of her. As she chanted the Sheheheyanu blessing her eyes welled with tears. When again would she have both her daughters with her?

Then the men lay on the couches and the women arranged themselves on the cushions around the perimeter of the room. Hayyim surveyed the room with satisfaction. As always Hadassah had prepared the room perfectly; he could not find any fault in the decorations. It never ceased to amaze him that his haggadah appeared at his place every year.

"Where did it hide the rest of the year? How blessed I am by my wife," he thought as he looked at her across the room. "Our children are healthy and respectful; our home is well appointed and always full of hospitality; and our relationship respectful." Then his gaze swept over his guests and he was thankful the idle conversation was over as that had not gone well earlier.

The entire Vide family absorbed the experience. Most of the seders that they had been to had been hurried affairs late at night performed by people who barely knew what they were doing. Here the participants relaxed and Hayyim understood the significance of the seder story. He explained it for everyone to understand, even the toddler Rachamim. As the Hebrew and Aramaic continued, with interruptions in Yevanic and Spanish by the various men to explain the service, the Vides became overwhelmed. In a peculiar way they had been slaves, too. Like the ancient Hebrews, they had been forced to give up their personal freedoms. Like the ancient Hebrews, they had fled their homeland with nothing of value, only their clothes, and wandered the world.

Clara listened attentively. For her, seder was always filled with wonder. As the kind Kyries Hayyim and Jacob explained the stories and symbols and her brother and cousin translated, she realized how close this story was to her own. The beauty of the shining silver on the tables, embroidered cloths and elaborate carpets around the room, fantastic chanting, and exotic smells from the kitchen practically sent her into a trance. She could not remember any experience so marvelous.

Rebecca was too nervous to focus on the seder. She closed her eyes and listened to Jacob's voice. Then she would open them and check her mother-in-law's face—was she satisfied? Then she would look at her mother—did she look pleased? The seder service was simply background noise to her.

Rahel was always fascinated by the service, the combination of recitation and singing, the story itself. This time, along with listening to her father explain the meanings of the story of the Hebrews' escape from Egyptian slavery, she listened to Jacob's. As they chanted, Rahel studied the faces of their guests. She noticed how Clara was so intent on listening and understanding and how Miguel and David became quieter and sadder.

At the beginning Miguel and José had participated eagerly, reciting the blessings and joining the story-telling and the songs. However, as the telling of the Exodus story continued, they grew quieter and quieter.

Finally Jacob turned to them and asked, "Why are you so quiet? We are here to celebrate how lucky we are."

José was thoughtful and then responded in his broken Greek, "We are more thankful than you can imagine. We are lucky to be here under the kind Sultan, to be here in this prosperous city, to be here in this generous home, but so many of our family and friends died before we got here. How can we not be sad for them? For their fates? For them never knowing the joy of being a Jew in public? I do not think my father or uncle ever went to a seder in a house where the windows were open and the songs were sung with passionate loud voices. For them, this holiday was about hope in the future, not thankfulness for a past act."

At that moment, Dinah entered the room with the first course of dinner—the eggs dyed in red onionskins.

Hayyim paused for a moment, "Come my friends and family, let us drink a toast to those who sacrificed so that their children could be free from the Pharaoh." And everyone, even Dinah, paused for a sip of wine. Miguel tried to remember what his father looked like as he drank his. Clara was introspective for the moment; she did not remember her parents or uncle. However, she had heard enough about them to know that they were honest religious people and wondered what they would think of this experience. José raised his glass high with a glad face and sad eyes because he remembered his father enough to miss him. Teresa and Maria toasted their loved ones and their luck with tears streaming down their faces; the mix of strong emotions, joy and sadness, and much wine was almost too much to bear.

After the first course was eaten, Hadassah and Rebecca rose from their places to serve the rest of the meal, beginning with chicken matzah soup. As they met in the kitchen, each smiled to the other.

Rebecca asked, "Manna, do you think Kyria Miriam likes me? Do you think she likes the food?" She was still terribly nervous that something would go wrong and her future would be destroyed.

Hadassah smiled and gently responded, "She seems very happy. Now take this tray in."

When Mimi fell asleep, Rahel helped them. When he was born and she was seven, Rahel felt important taking care of Mimi during seder. However, in the last year, he had become more independent and trustworthy and she realized it was not necessary to be that protective. That was when the compromise had been arranged—when he fell asleep, she could help serve. Now, again, Rahel felt important. All the more so, because she knew next year, her mother would rely upon her help as Rebecca would not be there. They pattered back and forth between the kitchen and seder refilling serving trays, making sure the men's plates were full, and only last making sure the women's plates were full.

After dessert was served and the afikoman eaten, but before the closing blessings, Hadassah sent Rahel to bed, "Off my child, it is well past your bed time."

"But Mother," protested Rahel, "I want to stay up. I want to sing the songs." Did not her mother understand? She was not a baby any longer. Besides, she wanted to study José more. He was exotic and smart and totally different from anyone she had met before.

"Maybe next year. You are almost asleep. I do not want you to break a tray. Take Mimi to his bed and off you go," responded her mother. There was no arguing with her mother, so off she went.

Rebecca watched Rahel go to bed with a twinge of jealousy. She was exhausted. Her day had started early and the stress and excitement of impressing her future husband and mother-in-law had drained her energy. However, she also felt pity for her sister that she was not a woman yet, only a girl, and so could not stay up.

Rahel went sadly to Mimi's room, "How unfair life is. I am old enough to stay up. My mother does not understand!" She continued this argument in her head even as she fell asleep in her best clothes next to Rachamim in his bed.

Even after the blessing closing the meal, the seder continued and Hadassah and Rebecca followed the same path between the two rooms, joining in the songs as they carried trays and dishes back to the kitchen. Rebecca quickly forgot about Rahel's trials as she imagined her own seder. She would arrange the formal room the way she liked; she would address the servants; she would cook the lamb the way her mother taught her.

Hayyim, David, Mordechai, and Jacob sang the songs loudly and joyfully. They blessed the wine with fervor. Miguel and José were both impressed with the power of the ceremony. The way in which their hosts related to the story and made it theirs, even though they had never experienced true oppression, made the Exodus story all the more potent to these newly freed young men.

All this was amazing to Clara. She desperately wanted to share her views with someone, but she knew she should not.

"How fascinating," Clara said to herself. "I wonder if men and women talk in private, or they never communicate about more than refilling their wine cup." However, she did enjoy the seder. The most amazing part of the experience was the joy. To her, seder had always been somewhat magical and scary because it was done secretly in the dark. It had never occurred to her that seder could be slow, careful, and joyous.

When the seder had concluded, near midnight, Hayyim thanked his guests, "To celebrate freedom as we do during Passover, is important. It reminds us of what we've gained and what we have. Each of you has made this evening a momentous event. It would not have been the same without you. I wish you peace and happiness. Next year in Jerusalem!" They all repeated this final sentence, yawned, and stood.

Chapter
12

Once they were in the hall, Rebecca whispered, "Did it all seem okay to you?"

"Did what seem okay?" asked her mother somewhat distractedly and very tired.

"The seder? Was it alright? Was Kyrio Jacob impressed? Were they upset that the others were here?" asked Rebecca breathlessly.

Hadassah thought for only a moment. "What was there not to be impressed by? Almost all the food was eaten, so it must have been good. Everyone ate, drank, and is leaving tired." And having come to her conclusion and the front room, Hadassah deemed their conversation was done. The mother and daughter returned the outerwear to the Vide family.

Miguel and José thanked Hayyim, David, and Mordechai profusely for the invitation. They nodded curtly to Jacob, whose derogatory remarks they had overheard earlier. Hadassah and Rebecca returned to them their feraçes and to the women their feraçes and peçes. Clara was exhausted, but excited. With the exotic food and four glasses of wine inside her, she could barely stay awake. Desperately she wished her Greek was better so that she could have spoken with Rahel. As she put on her feraçe, she looked wistfully around her. There was so much to see. What did the rest of the house look like? But it was late and, apparently, girls never spoke in this home. The Vide family borrowed a lantern to light their way home and left the house. Despite the hour, the streets were fairly busy as other seders where finishing and those guests were returning home, as well. Laughter and chatter filled the streets. The Vide family was silent not only because they were tired, but because the experience had overwhelmed them. They had seen the passion of the seder for people who were not closely connected to hatred and persecution.

When the door shut behind the Vides, Mordechai and Jacob immediately relaxed.

"Hayyim," said Jacob unable to contain himself, "that was an interesting experiment. I'm not sure I would have had the courage to hire a Spaniard, much less invite him to my house. However, we all know you to be a generous man."

Jacob thanked Hayyim again and helped his mother rise from the couch where she had been dozing. He smiled gently at Rebecca as she handed him his feraçe and admired the way she helped his mother wrap herself in the peçe. Miriam kissed Rebecca on the cheek in thanks and Rebecca blushed modestly.

When they had left with a borrowed lantern, Hadassah sent Rebecca, David, and Mordechai to bed.

As the three went to bed, Rebecca asked her brothers in the midst of a yawn, "Do you think they liked me? Not the Vides, who cares about the Vides. I mean Jacob and Miriam?" But the brothers were too tired to answer.

Hayyim sighed contentedly and said, "Thank you again, good wife. As always, a wonderful feast. Now go to bed and clean in the morning."

Hadassah laughed. They played this game every year. "Husband. Go to bed and let me clean before the work doubles," she cackled. He listened to her advice, as always, and fell asleep hearing her carrying dishes across the courtyard to the kitchen.

Chapter

13

On the first day of Passover, the day following the seder, Clara sat at the window in thought. A number of times her brother tried to interrupt her revelry, but it did not work.

After about an hour, Clara turned to her aunt, "Tía Maria, we will never have a life like Rebecca and Rahel's, will we?"

"We did once, Clara, even grander. But I doubt we will again," answered her aunt gently.

"I will not have a dowry," Clara said sadly. "We have no money. I should start a business. Other women here have businesses. I heard the older women discussing them last night." Now her voice seemed alive.

Maria looked at her niece with love and wonder. She seemed to have grown up in the last day, "And what business are you going to do? You cannot open a store on the street; women here do not do that. You cannot peddle; our family does not stoop to such measures."

"Do you remember when I was little you taught me to sculpt in clay? I know I've seen such items done in marzipan. Why can I not do that?" asked Clara.

"That is a wonderful idea," declared Maria.

"I want to start today. We owe David's family much. Let me start with a present for them."

"I can think of nothing better," Teresa declared. "José, take these coins, go to the Muslim part of town and buy some marzipan. Do not tell anyone anything other than you are taking a walk. This is to Judaism a holy day."

José left showing his displeasure. He felt torn about his task. Having rediscovered his Judaism, he wished to follow the laws and not carry

75

money or conduct business on this important day. However, his grandmother was the power in his family and no one dared argue with her. Besides, as with everyone they knew, he could refuse Clara nothing. He returned an hour later with marzipan of all colors.

"How wonderful!" exclaimed Clara when he came home with these goodies. Immediately, she sat down at the table. She had cleared it and cleaned it already. Clara's first few figures were rough and uneven. Slowly, she got used to the marzipan and how it softened as she molded it, the delicate touch she had to use, and what shapes it would not hold.

As her family watched in amazement, Clara began to create a delicate white basket that looked as though it had been woven out of reeds. Through the rest of the afternoon, Clara created exquisite delicate shapes.

Finally, Teresa came over to her and put a firm hand on her shoulder and announced, "Dearest Granddaughter, it is far too dark to work. Your eyes will be ruined. Here is a damp, clean cloth. Cover your creations until morning." With that, she handed Clara the cloth and helped her clean the table. The family ate their meal in their laps so as not to disturb Clara's work.

The next morning, Clara began her work as soon as the light came through the window. She only ate breakfast at the insistence of her aunt and refused to stop again until dark, by that time she had finished two complete works of art. Carefully, she wrapped each in a clean white cloth tied at the top with thread. Each was an elegant little bundle.

"Miguel, come here," Clara commanded. Miguel came over amazed at her new found authority. "Take these to Kyrio Hayyim tomorrow when you go to work. Make sure he knows that one is to go home to Kyria Hadassah. If you can, see if one can stay in the store. That way, people will see it and ask about it and I can sell some." Miguel simply nodded; there seemed little else he could do since his sister had made up her mind. He was amazed at how she had already worked out the start of her business.

Chapter

14

Hayyim kept the business closed for the next two days to observe the festival. On the third, he reopened. Muslims and Christians were waiting outside his door. Some complained that this was the third day they had arrived to do business with him. He smiled compassionately, explained there had been a holiday, and was twice as gracious.

Miguel arrived a few minutes later with two small bundles.

David asked anxiously about them, but all Miguel would say was, "Now is not the time."

"Miguel, David, I have a special task for you today," said Hayyim. The boys looked up expectantly. "It seems that there are rats nibbling the fabrics. Cut the nibbled bits out and see if you can find the little beasts. Check every bolt of fabric." They dutifully did their job, enjoying something different to do.

"Miguel, look," shouted David. "There are the footprints of the fabled lion."

Miguel looked and saw only the droppings of a rat, but he leapt over the chair, knocking it down in the process, and crawled along the trail like a hunter seeking his prey. A Christian customer nearly tripped over him.

"Boys," boomed Hayyim, "this is a business, not an expedition to discover new animals to amuse the sultan."

"Yes, sir," was their quick response, and so the hunt ended.

Finally, it was lunch and the men cleared a low table and pulled up some low stools. Most shopkeepers come spring would shut their shops for an extended lunch at home with a nap after because come the summer this was the only way to cope with the heat; however, Hayyim never did. He claimed he had far too much work and might miss a customer. In reality, he liked having the quiet time in the shop and did not particularly enjoy going home to be around women more than he had to. As much as he admired and appreciated his wife and adored his daughters, he felt most comfortable in the shop with his sons. Thus, the four made themselves as comfortable as possible in the crowded, hot shop.

Dinah arrived with a basket.

Once she placed it on the table, Miguel stood, bowed to her, and said, as he placed one of the bundles in her hands, "Be so kind, Kyria Dinah, as to present this gift to your mistress with the compliments of my aunt and grandmother." Dinah blushed. No one had ever before spoken to her with such respect. Not that anyone was disrespectful, but it was quite clear in how she was addressed by others that she held a lesser place in society. She was addressed merely as Dinah and on her rare visits to her parents as "Eldest daughter." Miguel saw her blush and felt repentant. He had not meant to embarrass her; he wanted to honor her. His aunt and grandmother had taught him that servants were important members of society as well. She turned to Hayyim with a questioning look.

Hayyim gave her a paternal smile, "Go on, Dinah. Make sure my wife receives the gift of the Kyries Vides." Then he turned to Miguel, "Your aunt and grandmother are most kind."

"Oh, no, Kyrio Hayyim," responded Miguel. "Your family was most kind to us to invite us for seder." Then he opened the other bundle. David, Mordechai, and Hayyim gasped as the fabric opened like a flower. Inside was a small basket containing the most exquisite tiny flowers and miniature fruits.

Mordechai reached out to touch it, "What a marvel. Where did your aunt find such flowers and fruit? They seem so real."

Miguel smiled, "This is marzipan. Clara is very talented. Once when she was little she made herself a farm filled with animals and soldiers for me." The four admired the art as they ate.

When they finished, there was an awkward moment. Miguel had watched Clara spend two days creating these baskets begging for a bite. Of course, he would never begin the basket; that would be rude considering it was a gift to the family and his sister had asked him to make sure it was on display. David and Mordechai had never seen a creation like this and could not decide if they should eat it or not.

Finally, Hayyim spoke with care; he wanted to thank this family and not insult the artist, "Miguel, your sister's work is beyond words. This is too beautiful to eat. Let us leave it here on the table for our customers to admire, and later we will take it home and share this with the women." While the three younger men were disappointed with the comment since they had all wanted a bite, they could not argue with such a truthful statement. Even though Miguel was disappointed, he was also pleased. Clara's understanding of people and business was amazing, especially for someone with no experience. Her work would be in the store for everyone to admire.

For the rest of the afternoon, the customers came in and admired the display. A few asked about it and they were referred to Miguel. Miguel was amazed. A number of them inquired about getting a similar piece, and he promised to get back to them once he discussed it with his sister. Every time someone asked, he smiled. They thought he was being kind. In actuality, he was smiling to himself at how clever Clara was. Already she had a number of orders.

As soon as Hayyim had told her to go home, Dinah did and brought her bundle carefully back to the house. She found Hadassah in the courtyard cleaning beans and singing while Rahel and Mimi played catch.

"Mistress, the Vide family sent this gift to you in thanks for the seder," she said as she gently put the package on the ground at Hadassah's feet.

Hadassah brushed her hands off and untied the thread. The fabric fell open and there, in the sun, glittered a basket — a duplicate to the one that the men were soon to open.

Mimi's ball bounced dangerously close to Hadassah and the basket and she yelled, "Play on the other side of the courtyard!!" He ran to get the ball and stopped, momentarily, to look at the basket.

"Pretty basket," he cooed.

"What basket?" asked Rahel, as she wandered over to see.

"I'm not sure it is a basket," commented Hadassah. "The fruit are made of …" and she touched one, "marzipan," she said in disbelief. "This is incredible. I have never seen anything like it."

At that moment, Rebecca entered the courtyard with a basin of water to begin washing the rice for dinner. "Mother, what is that? Did someone send it as a wedding gift?" she asked ever eager to be the center of attention.

"No, silly," retorted Rahel. "The Vides sent it to say thank you. It is beautiful, yes?"

Rebecca's smile washed away. She had hoped her contact with the Vides was over. Even though they dressed properly if poorly, it was clear they were uncomfortable with proper society. That old woman, the grandmother, spent the entire evening rearranging the pillows she was leaning on as if they were not comfortable. And the other two women sat through the entire ceremony without speaking. They must have known that they had to participate? How could they not know the service? Rebecca had been embarrassed for them and by them.

Mimi looked at it hungrily, "Can we eat it then?" And immediately his hand reached for the basket.

Hadassah smacked his little hand, "No. We cannot eat it. We do not know how kosher their house is. It is beautiful, however, so let us put it in the formal room to admire." With that she carefully picked up the basket, still sitting in the cloth, and carried it to the formal room leaving everyone else behind.

Rebecca had not moved. She was weighing her desire for copies of the edible artwork against her fear of the Spanish interlopers. After a moment, Rebecca followed her into the house. "Manna, Manna!" she called after her. It took only a moment to find her putting the basket on a low table in the corner of the room. "Manna …"

"Yes, dear. I did hear you calling me," responded Hadassah quietly.

"Could we get some baskets like this for my kiddushin?" questioned her oldest daughter.

"I doubt it. Unless we asked the Vide women to come to our kitchen and make them, so that I can make sure they keep kosher. I will think about it," and with that Hadassah closed the discussion. Rebecca knew that her mother really would think about this, consider whatever issues were relevant, and come up with a well thought out conclusion. She left the formal room satisfied.

Chapter
15

A bit over a month later, Shavuot arrived, and before the families went to their synagogues, they decorated their homes with bows of greenery. Hadassah and Dinah made a feast of kassata; leek and potato fritadas; and halva. Hayyim particularly liked the kassata. Across the city, the Vide women were making zucchini and eggplant fritadas, and rice pudding.

Once the festival was over, Hadassah became serious about her daughter's kiddushin. The dowry goods and price were agreed upon and finished. Rebecca was finishing her outfit for the kiddushin ceremony. With each stitch, Rebecca felt the moment of betrothal coming closer. At the same time, she was excited and nervous: excited to be a woman, nervous not to be a child; excited to have her own home, nervous to be a wife. What did she know of being a wife? Rebecca understood the daily routine, the role a wife plays in homemaking, and how to raise children, but what frightened her were the references to the "wifely duty." Nobody would explain any more than that. With that last thought, she looked down at her sewing. With a heavy sigh, she undid the last row of stitches. She had done them poorly because her mind was not on her work.

One evening not many days later, Mordechai was sent to the Vides' home. He did not want to go, but his father made it clear that his opinion about either the mission or the Vides was not relevant. He had been chosen to take the message. He was the oldest son.

David gave him directions.

"I wish I was going," he commented rather disappointedly.

"So do I," Mordechai answered quickly. "However, this is not a social call. It is business and you are not ready to negotiate a business contract." And so Mordechai set off on what he felt was this distasteful errand. He found the Vides' home rather easily, admitting to himself that his brother gave good directions. He stood outside the door for a moment collecting himself and then knocked.

José opened the door and stood there stunned for a moment. Mordechai was the last person he expected to see at his home. After the seder, Miguel had brought home more stories about how Romaniotes, including Mordechai, treated him at the store; their attitude was at best tolerant and civil, but far from friendly.

"Who is there?" asked his grandmother. Since José stood in front of the doorway, she could not see around him.

This brought him out of his shock long enough to bring the guest in, but he still could not speak.

"Please sit here," José finally croaked as he pulled out a stool. Then José and Miguel sat at the table with Maria and Teresa standing behind them. Clara looked up curiously and then returned to cleaning her table. She had learned enough of local custom to know she should not appear to be part of the discussion. Mordechai tried not to look uncomfortable.

He cleared his throat and looked at only José. "We would like to hire Clara to do some work for Rebecca's kiddushin."

Teresa smiled, so did Clara as she turned her head away from their guest.

José replied, "That is fine. What do you need?" They had agreed earlier that José would take care of the business, or appear to. The Vides were unsure exactly how much women could do in public, so José took over the negotiations of contracts for Clara's business. He knew better than to believe he was in charge. Clara was a strong woman, like his grandmother, and had proven already her business acumen.

Clara waited—she knew this would be a big order. It was also an important one because Señor Hayyim's family was a powerful one in the community. If she did well for this event, then her fortune in marzipan would be made.

"We would like 10 baskets of fruit and flowers like the ones Clara made as a gift for us," Mordechai replied firmly. "We want 10 boats with animals—like little Noah's arks." He was not pleased to be at the Vide home, nor did he like the idea of doing business with these Sephardim. His opinion, however, had not been requested. Rebecca had cajoled her parents into being the first in the community to have such an elegant and unusual display. Mordechai had also realized that for some reason his father had a soft spot for Miguel. So Rebecca did not have to work terribly hard to convince their father to offer some business to a member of Miguel's family. This did not make Mordechai happy. He wanted as little to do with these interlopers as possible. But having been well-trained by his father, he hid his feelings and conducted the business at hand.

"Of course," replied José.

Clara could barely contain herself with excitement. Already she was calculating how long it would take to make these baskets, and how much she would earn. Outwardly, however, she remained cool and quiet. She had no training in handling business matters like Mordechai, but she had intuition. She knew that if Mordechai knew how interested she really was he would negotiate her out of some good money, and they desperately needed every coin that any of them could earn.

Mordechai continued where he was interrupted, "and we would like her to make them at our house."

Teresa's face turned dark. "She will not stay there! Clara is MY granddaughter," she blurted out.

"Nor would we expect her to," Mordechai answered without looking at Teresa. His mother had warned him to reassure the family that they were not interested in taking Clara from them. No one in Hayyim's house was sure he or she wanted to know the Sephardim that well. She had also suggested that the Vides were not like them, and José was probably not in charge. Mordechai accepted this comment at face value without realizing how much control his mother had in the family. He believed his father was the ultimate force in the family. It did not occur to him that once the children were asleep, his parents argued through many disagreements. Mordechai, therefore, responded to Teresa's inappropriate outburst, though he could not bring himself to look at her.

"We simply want her to work in our house," he said, "not to live there."

José and Miguel looked at each other in confusion. What a strange request, Miguel thought. She was not a servant, but a businesswoman. While a servant would live in her employer's house, as a businesswoman she should be able to work in her own home. José's thoughts were very much the same. In a city where women are so protected by their families and the civil law, why should he be expected to allow his sister out of his house?

With that thought, José turned to Mordechai and asked, "Why can she not work here where she is comfortable and we will make sure her creations come to your house?"

Now Mordechai looked truly uncomfortable. It would insult these people that his mother did not trust them. No matter how he felt about the Vides, it went against his Jewish upbringing to shame anyone. His mother had agreed to allow Clara to create her artwork, but only in her home. There, she could guarantee that the edible art was kosher. He cleared his throat a number of times trying to find the answer.

"Well, we thought it might be easier for her since we have more room and we can buy and store her marzipan."

Clara stole up to her aunt. So far, no one had asked her opinion. Wasn't her opinion the one that really mattered?

She tugged on Maria's sleeve and whispered in her ear, "I'll go. It will be fun! I'll see how to keep kosher and run the house. I can even improve my Greek."

Maria looked down. The excitement shone in her niece's eyes. With a deep sigh, which was the only expression of her misgiving, Maria put her hand on her son's shoulder and gave a slight squeeze. José knew this signal.

He turned to Miguel and said, "I will let Clara go . …." Here he was interrupted by a quick squeal of joy from Clara. He gave her a dark look from his eyes as a reprimand with a smile on his lips as support, "… so long," he continued, "as you, Miguel, walk her to and fro every day when you go to work." Miguel nodded his assent.

Mordechai nodded his approval, pushed back his chair, and stood up relieved to be done with this unpleasant business. José did the same with very much the same feeling.

Mordechai announced to no one in particular, "Then we will see Clara tomorrow." He turned, went to the door, opened it, and left. Once he was outside the door, he brushed himself off. There was something about the Sephardim that made him feel dirty. When he was well down the street, he took a deep breath to clean his lungs. While his parents and sister would be pleased with the outcome of his negotiations, Mordechai was not so sure. This personal contact with the Spanish worried him, though he could not explain why.

Miguel could barely shut the door fast enough behind Mordechai.

"What good fortune for us all," he thought. "Clara's work will bring in some money and maybe we could afford a nicer home for our grandmother and aunt if her work becomes regular." He turned around to the very different expressions of his family.

Clara was aglow.

She could barely contain herself. "This is so exciting! Do you realize? Twenty pieces! That is so much money. Everyone should have new clothes. Even you, Abuela. Maybe I should save some for a dowry. Tía Maria, what do you think?"

Maria could not help but be infected by Clara's joy. "I think you need to stop chattering. Let us have the money in hand and then we will worry about what to spend and what to save. And please, little Clara, stop nagging about Abuela's clothes!"

Teresa was still worried.

"Why do you really think they want Clara at their home?" she asked as she sat down at the table. Her question was not addressed to anyone in particular and she did not expect an answer. Then she turned to Clara with a dark look, "And I heard your comments, Clara. What is there to learn in that home that is full of superstitious nonsense?" Here Señora Vide's anger started to rise, "I have taught you far more than those girls will ever know."

Clara cowered for a moment; then she stood tall and confident in her newfound maturity and place as a contributing member of the household.

"Abuela, you have taught me what a girl in Spain would need to know. But I am not a girl and I am not in Spain. Here life is different. I need to know how to be a Jewish woman—a Jewish wife. Can you teach me that? You say that the Jews here are superstitious and old fashioned. That may be, but if I am to live here as a Jew, I must do as they do. Here is my opportunity to learn without being noticed. I'll even get paid for it! Who will marry me if I cannot keep a proper home? Many of our fellow Sephardim are turning to the traditional ways which they learn from the Venetians. If I do not know the ways, who will have me?"

The room was silent. No one breathed. Never had anyone spoken to the matriarch in such a tone. Even Teresa was silent. Then she smiled. "Dearest Clara, I see much of your father in you. He too was eager and stubborn. What can I do? If I say no, we shall lose face since we've already said yes. And the money is needed. And saying no to this family will guarantee that there is no work among the local Jews. In many ways, you are right. There are things you need to know that I cannot teach you. You will need to find a husband. Go. Do well. Be what I taught you: honest, yet courteous; kind, gentle, and wise. Learn all that you can. But never forget who you are and where you came from."

Immediately, Clara returned to being a girl, ran to grandmother, and threw her arms around her neck.

"I will NEVER forget, Abuela," she promised. With that, the matriarch rose from the table with a power and grace that come only from age and experience, and walked to the window. She did not want anyone to see the emotional conflict in her face. Her children finally had the opportunity to be Jews freely, which was wonderful; yet she could not teach them, and that was heart wrenching. The life she once knew was dead. That was not really so bad, but would she ever find a place in the new world?

José and Miguel ran to the table and eagerly joined Clara in a discussion of the proposed project. How much material would Clara need? How much time? What would they spend the money on? Maria, on the other hand, watched her mother-in-law. She knew that voice and those words. Very much the same speech had been given to her husband and brother-in-law on the last night the family had been together and the brothers were deciding on joining a secret Jewish society. She had received the same speech when she had finally convinced Teresa to leave Spain and not be caught in the fires of the Inquisition. Maria knew what her mother-in-law was thinking: the world was changing and she could no longer control it. Maria felt much the same. She walked to the window and put her arm around the woman whom she considered to be her mother. Together they stared out into the street that was still so foreign to them and wondered, each to herself, if she would ever truly be part of it.

Chapter
16

___

Dutifully the next morning, Miguel walked his sister to the front door of Hayyim's house before he went to work in the store. Miguel had to nudge his sister along so that he would not be late. She stopped to look at everything: the displays in shop windows, the feraçe of an Ottoman woman toting two children, even a potted tree outside a door. Usually, he enjoyed his sister's curiosity, but he had no intention of ruining his reputation because of her naïveté.

On the other hand, Clara was nervous. She knew how proud Miguel was of his reputation at Kyrio Hayyim's store. She was equally as proud of it, but today everything seemed so interesting. As anxious as she was to start this job and see the inside of a Romaniote home, Clara was just as uneasy. Finally, after Miguel's endless nagging to hurry and Clara's seemingly insatiable curiosity, they arrived at a door. To Clara it seemed no different from any other entrance they had passed. Miguel knocked and when a hunchbacked woman opened the door, he left without saying a word to either woman. He had learned not to address the female servants in a house, and he really had nothing to say, especially since he was almost late to work. The woman stepped back from the door and motioned her to come in.

"Shalom," she said to Clara and led her through the courtyard to the kitchen in the back of the house. Clara looked all around her. First, she studied this woman. Obviously, she was a servant, but the hunchback's clothes were far more expensive and newer than her own. Everything that Clara saw was exotic and beautiful. The cushions on the benches, the carpets on the floors, even the plants in the courtyard. As Clara followed the serving woman through the courtyard away from the house, she wondered where they were going. Then in the back of the courtyard she saw a small stone structure standing all by itself and realized that it must be the kitchen.

Dinah entered the kitchen with Clara and said, "Kyria Hadassah, Despoynida Clara is here." Then she disappeared into another part of the house. The kitchen seemed huge to Clara. The idea of a room devoted entirely to cooking was something she vaguely remembered from her childhood; even so, when her aunt and grandmother still had servants she rarely went into the kitchen. At the end of the kitchen was a large oven. The sides of the room were fairly similar. Cupboards, cabinets, and counters lined the walls. Down the center of the room was a large wooden table with benches underneath.

Hadassah gave a small smile and brought Clara to the far end of the table, near the cellar.

"This is your spot. Do you understand?" she asked as she patted the table. Hadassah was careful to speak clearly and slowly to this girl. After all, she had no idea how much Yevanic she knew; their conversation before seder had been brief. Hadassah was very unsure whether Clara was a girl or a young woman. She looked no older than her younger daughter Rahel, but David had discovered she was nearer to Rebecca's age.

Clara nodded as she wondered what this woman thought of her. Clara studied Hadassah. She was a pretty woman with a wrinkled face and a few teeth missing—not an uncommon trait for a woman nearing middle age. She was plump and of middle height, and quite obviously in charge of what was going on around her.

Then Hadassah turned toward the courtyard and said, "Come, come here and see." They crossed the courtyard to a small room where the shutters were closed tightly. When their eyes adjusted, Hadassah took Clara by the hand and turned her to one corner of the small room and there was an open crate filled with marzipan in a rainbow of colors.

Clara was thrilled, "Oh how wonderful! The colors are beautiful." Then she stopped when Hadassah's blank face looked back at her. She had been speaking in Spanish. "They are pretty. Thank you," Clara said slowly in her broken Greek. Hadassah smiled and left her in the room to begin. At first, Clara could not take her eyes off the crate. She had never imagined so many vivid colors to work with. Once she accepted that, she turned to examine the rest of the room. This small space was neatly organized with large jars of oil and wine on the floor against the walls, and on the shelves were jars of cheese, clusters of dried herbs, tubs of butter and rendered animal fat, dyes, and items Clara could not name. There were enormous barrels filled with sacks of flour—an interesting assortment of flours. Clara could barely comprehend these vast quantities of food. When she heard voices in the courtyard, she tore her eyes from the store room and returned to the marzipan. She grabbed a hunk of the white and holding it in her skirt she returned to the kitchen.

Clara worked diligently for a week creating baskets filled with fruit and boats filled with animals. While she did so, she watched Dinah and Hadassah kasher the meat, cook the meals, organize the dishes, and grind the herbs for medical problems. She discovered that Hadassah was well respected among the Romaniotes for her ability to cure certain ailments, and that servants and ladies from the community often came to request something from her. Sometimes they would come alone and describe the problem, sometimes they would bring a sick child, and sometimes they would arrive and beg Kyria Hadassah to come with them. On these occasions, Hadassah would take a large clean cloth and gather a number of different herbs to take with her. Clara watched Rebecca study her mother as she mixed poultices for bruises and blessed talismans for the safety of those she loved. Many of the herbal mixes Clara knew or knew variations of, but the talismans were new to her. Teresa called them all superstitious nonsense.

Clara studied Rebecca, too, and grew to admire her. They were almost the same age and yet their lives were so different. Rebecca had her mother, and though Clara had never been treated as anything less than a daughter by her aunt, she still wondered what it was like to have a mother. Clara could barely remember having anything she wanted.

Her memories, while filled with the love of her family, also contained the many deprivations of sinking into poverty. In this kitchen, not only was the food abundant, but the variety was immense. It occurred to Clara that in many ways, she related more to Dinah, who did the menial work in the kitchen and wore the hand-me-down clothes of Kyria Hadassah, just as Clara wore whatever used clothes she could buy in the market. Clara wanted to chat and ask questions, but she was still afraid. Her fear came from the unknown, as well as being uncomfortable speaking Greek. However, when she was spoken to she always answered politely.

Rahel desperately wanted to talk to Clara.

"Clara is hired to work, not to chat," the girls had been told. "However, she is to be treated respectfully, just like any other employee in the house."

"But there are so many things I want to know," whined Rahel. "How do they celebrate the holidays? What was Spain like? Why did they leave? And how do you pretend to be something you are not? This is not fair!"

"Fair or not, I do not want you speaking with her. She is here to work." That was her mother's final word.

However, Rahel watched Clara when she was not aware of it. It was quite clear to Rahel Clara was just as anxious to talk.

Rebecca was not interested in Clara as an individual. She saw her as the person who produced what she wanted for her kiddushin. She was polite to Clara, but relatively cold. It was quite clear to Rebecca that Clara was simple. She knew almost nothing about keeping kosher, she could barely speak a complete sentence, and she never knew what prayer to say for any occasion, such as seeing a rainbow or hearing a clap of thunder.

Chapter
17

Once the final negotiations were settled on the order for Rebecca's kiddushin party, the Vide family decided to invest in another table, so that they would not disturb the creations Clara made at home and could enjoy a meal. When Clara was home, she was working as well because she had orders from others in Thessaloniki. All of this good fortune made Miguel happy.

He discussed it with Clara one day as they walked to work together. "Clara, what shall we do with our money? Someday soon Abuela and Tía Maria will not have to worry about money. What should we treat them to?"

"Oh, that is simple, Miguel," replied Clara. "New clothes, not new for them like what we have, but new ones made for them. And treats, some food that they love from Spain that is hard to find."

Miguel laughed, "Always clothes, dear sister. You are so worried about clothes."

David was depressed. His sister would soon be betrothed. Watching the items being prepared for the kiddushin only made that reality weigh more heavily on him. This was something that Miguel could not understand. "After all," he argued again and again with David, "it is only the kiddushin, the engagement. It will be fun! A big party. It's not as though they're getting married right away," he thought to himself. David grumbled and walked off. Even he could not quite figure out why he was so upset.

Both Hadassah's and Hayyim's extended family knew the date; as did Jacob's extended family. The group was not as big as one might expect because not only were Hayyim and Jacob cousins, but so were

95

Hayyim and Hadassah. A few of Hayyim's best customers and Jacob's friends were invited as well. The result was that almost the entire Romaniote community in the city was going to watch Jacob and Rebecca become betrothed, along with a few Venetians and Ashkenazim. Even so, despite repeated attempts by David, Hayyim would not allow the Vide family to be invited.

"But father," David argued two days before the event, "the Vides are our friends!"

"No, David," responded his father. "Miguel may be your friend, but he is my employee."

"Father," retorted David. "You invited them to seder two months ago."

"You are correct, but we invite many people to our house to eat on holidays. They are not always our friends. Some are needy members of the community. Some are distant relatives. Some are Jews passing through the port. That is tzedakah," replied Hayyim.

David drew a slow breath. He knew that this was his last chance to get his best friend invited. "Father, may I invite just Miguel?"

Hayyim's first inclination was to refuse again. Jacob, while polite at seder, had made it clear that he was not pleased by his future father-in-law's choice of guests. The Spanish Jews were not welcome into the existing community, according to Jacob's philosophy. But Hayyim knew how close David and Miguel had become and wondered, since the Spanish Jews were an overwhelming majority of the Jewish population, if it might be wise to invite them.

"Very well, you may bring Miguel to the kiddushin. But, David, do not flaunt him around our guests."

David contemplated this request. His father obviously was not pleased by the idea of having Miguel there, but David was.

"Of course, Father. Thank you!" Quickly his father's concerns left his mind as he rushed away to the Vide home to tell Miguel the news. Since the first time he had been there, David had become less shocked by the role that Theresa played in the family. He had come to realize that his mother played much the same role, although she did it differently. There were times when Hadassah made decisions about how the family would approach a situation, and she handled her dowry investments fairly wisely. There always seemed to be a little extra for special items for the children or Dinah. However, while Hadassah was quiet and did not speak in front of men other than her husband, sons, and brothers, Teresa discussed everything from politics to cooking with anyone who was available. The Sephardim visited each other, just as the Romaniotes did, and Teresa and Maria's house, though only a room, had become a popular place to visit at any time during the day. David could not become accustomed to the way that Spanish men and women addressed each other; friends used familiar terms of address of the sort that Romaniotes used only with family members. But he liked being there and listening to the stories people told in his newfound Ladino. With Miguel's tutoring, David had become quite fluent in the language he once thought was Spanish. Miguel had corrected him early on in their lessons and explained that he was teaching a language similar to Spanish, but spoken only by the Jews.

When David arrived, Juan, his wife Eva, and their baby were visiting. David grabbed Miguel's arm and dragged him into a corner by the cook stove.

"Miguel, come to my sister's kiddushin in two days. You're right it will be great fun!" David whispered a little too loudly. Everyone in the room heard the invitation, but everyone ignored it. Along with knowing it was not their place to comment on the personal life of someone else, even if it did affect their lives, they had learned to live in a confined space and to pretend not to know what was going on around them. Soon enough, the answer to the invitation would make it to every home and the community would be able to comment on it.

José heard the invitation, but said nothing. It had taken very little time for Miguel to assert his independence once he had started earning some money. After an hour or so David excused himself and returned home in a much happier mood. Shortly thereafter, Juan and Eva left and the Vides were on their own. As had become their custom, they sat around the table chatting with the glow of one candle flickering.

Señora Vide turned to Miguel and asked, "What brought David along this evening? The two of you seemed quite secretive."

"Abuela, David came to invite me to Rebecca's kiddushin," Miguel replied.

Clara's eyes lit up, "We're invited to the kiddushin? How exciting. Abuela, may I buy some new nalin?" Immediately her mind started working on how long it would take to clean her good clothes.

Once Clara took a breath, Miguel jumped in, "Clara, the invitation was for me – not the family." He had not meant his comment to hurt his sister's feelings; rather, he felt he was stating a fact.

Tears welled up in Clara's eyes and then she covered her face with her hands.

She sobbed, "I did all that work for Rebecca's party! I want to go! I want to see!" Miguel did not understand why his sister was acting so babyish.

Maria put her arm across the girl's shoulders, "Clara, you were paid for your work. That is the role of a craftsman. You sell your goods."

"But I never get to go anywhere! This will be a big party and I want to see it," pouted Clara, once again a little girl.

"Don't be sad, Clara," Miguel said, his eyes twinkling. "One day, you too will have a wedding, with a kiddushin, and a nisuin, a marriage ceremony. And after you are properly married, you will leave us happily to live with your new husband."

Clara looked at him, and shook her head. "Don't make fun," she said bitterly.

Very quietly and gently José asked Miguel, "Are you going to go?" He had terribly mixed feelings about allowing his young cousin to attend the event. Part of him was pleased that Miguel had been accepted into the local community, even if it was only by one family. However, the other part of him was nervous that Miguel would lose his sense of self.

"Of course, cousin," Miguel quickly replied. "Why shouldn't I? David asked me. Surely, that means his family approves. I just do not understand why we all were not invited. From what I've heard around the store, most of the local Jewish community will be there."

José looked quickly at his grandmother and then his mother. With a sad look, Maria nodded ascent to her son.

Speaking softly, José began, "Miguel, we are not all invited because we are not welcome here. No other member of our Jewish community is—only the Romaniote. Did you not hear the comments Señor Jacob made before he knew we were in Señor Hayyim's house? The Romaniotes do not like us—they are not even sure we are Jews."

"How can you say that?" Clara burst out. "Of course, we're Jews."

"Clara! Let your cousin finish!" commanded the matriarch.

"No, Abuela. She is right. We know who we are. Our parents, grandparents, and great-grandparents made hard choices to save lives during the Inquisition. They hid their Jewish identity, and had to stop living Jewish lives. And now, because some of us are less knowledgeable about Jewish practices and rituals, because we may be less stringent about observing some of the laws, because we do things differently—the Jews here in Thessaloniki dislike us as a group." José paused. "Miguel, you are lucky. You and David have made a friendship. Most of us are not so lucky, nor do I believe we ever will be. Nurture this. Go, but beware. Realize that you may be welcomed only by David."

Silence filled the room. It hung heavily as everyone weighed the words José had spoken. José studied his cousin's face. This was not the world either had hoped for. Their whispered dreams shared in bed at night had been of riches, comfort, and acceptance. Instead, they had found themselves struggling to support their family and embroiled in another controversy. While this one did not involve their physical well-being, it did encompass their cultural future. Maria hung her head and Teresa rested her face in her hands. Neither wanted the "children" to see the defeat and sadness in their faces. They felt as if their battle for the family's survival was over. Clara was simply dumbfounded. Her world had always been one of brightness; her family had carefully shielded her from the darkness that had clouded their lives. This was the first time she was presented with a gray and uncertain future. Miguel looked at each member of his family. While he listened carefully to José's remarks, he refused to believe them. Here they were free to be Jews—everything else was unimportant. He, a poor exile, had been invited to be part of a major family's celebration. They sat in silence until the candles burned low. The air hung heavy with feelings: Clara's disappointment, Miguel's elation, the deep concern and defeated sadness of Teresa, Maria, and José. Finally, the flames flickered and went out, a faint spiral of smoke rising from the burnt-out wick. The family rose, and went to bed.

Chapter

18

The night before the kiddushin, Rebecca and Rahel lay in bed together, unable to sleep. A great change in their lives had begun in the morning, but neither was quite sure how to talk about it. Finally, Rahel broke the silence, "What time will you leave in the morning?"

"For the mikveh?" responded Rebecca. "When Manna finishes breakfast. She told me not to come to the kitchen because I cannot eat until after the betrothal ceremony." The girls lay quietly for a moment. "Did you finish the embroidering?"

"Yes, Rebecca," was Rahel's exasperated reply. "This morning." Another long pause followed. "It will be strange not having you here anymore after tomorrow."

"It will be strange not being here anymore," replied her sister. "But I will not be far away, only down the road. You are welcome at any time, after all, you are my sister."

"Will things be different? I mean between us?" Rahel asked.

Rebecca rolled over and held Rahel close, "What could be different? You are my sister and always will be." And with that, they fell asleep, one embracing the other.

On the morning of the kiddushin, Hadassah left Dinah in charge of the kitchen as her mother, sisters, sisters-in-law, and cousins started arriving with specialties for the festivities. Hadassah took Rebecca to the mikvah. There Miriam, Rebecca's soon to be mother-in-law, and the attendants met them. The women carefully undressed Rebecca, trimmed her fingernails and toenails; brushed her hair; and whispered wishes, advice, and blessings in her ears. Rebecca thought it sounded like the whispers of angels—just barely audible words that did not quite make sense. When she was ready, the attendants took Rebecca into the mikvah, a pool of cool, clear water. She was instructed to walk slowly into the ritual bath and immerse herself in it completely in the water. When she emerged, an attendant recited the blessing and Rebecca repeated it. She immersed herself in the waters a total of three times. Then the women escorted Rebecca from the bath, dried her, and dressed her. Hadassah and Miriam walked Rebecca back to her father's house to be dressed in her kiddushin clothes. Along the way, family and friends greeted them with blessings and good wishes. The trio made their way through the streets as if they were a grand procession for a princess.

Through this process, Rebecca was silent. Her mind was a jumble of fear, excitement, and joy. She was thankful that her mother could go with her to the mikvah—some of her friends had no mother and went with an aunt, cousin, or worse, stepmother. The ritual cleansing seemed to take forever. Once it was done, however, it seemed too fast. How kind the attendants were. How gentle. How sweet her mother-in-law was. Every step brought her closer to the ultimate moment. It seemed so long ago that her father had begun the marriage negotiations. Was it really only eight months? Hadassah escorted a very quiet Rebecca home again to dress her in her finest dowry outfit.

When everyone was ready, Hayyim led the family to the entrance of the synagogue. As they strolled down the street, people showered blessings upon Rebecca and her family. Invited guests joined the family en route to the synagogue. More and more people came, until there was a grand procession of brightly colored feraçes punctuated with loud voices of people greeting one another. As the parade neared the synagogue, it gradually grew quiet until it fell silent. There, Jacob bar Isaac and his brothers-in-law met his mother, Hayyim, and Hayyim's family. There was quite a crowd assembled to celebrate the union of these two much-loved and respected families.

Rebecca saw almost none of this spectacle. She was in a trance. She had been fasting and was feeling both fearful and excited about the events unfolding around her. Going to the mikvah that morning had only emphasized the changes that were rapidly taking place in her life. It seemed that all this fuss was happening to someone else and she was watching it from afar. Now, at the entrance to the synagogue, everything in her life was about to transform.

Miguel had arrived, and stood quietly to the side in the doorway. David's heart raced. Spying Miguel, he quickly walked over to his side.

The ceremony began with the reading of the dowry agreement. The crowd was hushed, impressed with the extensive list of goods, and anticipating seeing them on display during the celebration later on. Once the reading was completed, the couple was placed standing next to one another. Rebecca heard none of the ceremony. Her mind was spinning from the excitement. The stefana was placed on their heads.

Miguel leaned over to David, "What are those?"

David was a bit taken aback, "The stefana?" he whispered. "Don't you know what they are?"

Miguel shook his head.

"The two hoops represent that the bride and groom are now the queen and king of their new home. They are tied together to show that they are now one. The stefena are swapped on their heads to indicate that each is now part of the other."

"It is a strange custom," was Miguel's response.

"Strange?" questioned David. "Even the Christians do it. It is an ancient custom."

They returned their attention to the ceremony in time to hear most of the seven wedding blessings recited.

Rahel was awed by the whole process. She had been to many kiddushin, as her extended family was large and her father was an important businessman. But this kiddushin was different. This was her sister's. It did not seem real until the stefana were placed on Rebecca's and Jacob's heads. The two rings, beautifully decorated with flowers and ribbons, were tied together, representing the bond that Rebecca and Jacob would now share—a bond that she would never have with her sister. Rahel shook her head as if to dust off the thoughts and looked around the crowd as a diversion.

As Miguel listened to the blessing, he suddenly grew tense. Turning to David, he demanded, "Is this a wedding, or a betrothal?"

"A betrothal." David whispered. "You see, there is no huppah. And the ketubbah has not been read."

"But those are the wedding blessings. I know, I heard them when Juan and Eva were married," returned Miguel. Another member of the crowd turned and hushed them. The boys remained silent until the blessings were finished being chanted.

"Why are the wedding blessings sung?" Miguel repeated, confused by the use of the wedding blessings at a kiddushin.

"How else would it be?" David inquired, also confused. "The couple is now betrothed and will be married within the year."

Once the ceremony ended, the crowd dispersed, and poured out into the street and on to Hayyim's house for the celebration. Miguel and David joined the crowd. David exchanged cheery greetings with his family and friends as Miguel grew more sullen.

Miguel really didn't understand. The ceremony was a mixture of kiddushin and nisuin. The announcement for the wedding had been made. The list of the dowry publicized. But why had the couple been blessed with the Sheva Brachot? Why were they being escorted as a couple to the party? He felt more and more uncomfortable the nearer they got to the reception.

Chapter
19

Rebecca was entirely overwhelmed by her kiddushin. Sitting among the women in her mother's house she realized she was a guest there for the first time. Being treated as a princess with everyone serving her had seemed like a wonderful dream, but now it made her feel uncomfortable. She desperately wanted to bring the serving trays around the room. It had been her job only yesterday. She was glad Jacob was with the men, so that he couldn't see her being uncomfortable. He certainly wouldn't feel out of place; he was used to being waited on.

Dinah offered her a sweet from a tray.

"No Dinah, no more. I'm quite full from all the other treats you have given me. Thank you." "How odd," she thought, "to be a guest in this house—my home, until this morning." "Thank you, Thea. You are most kind," she said to an aunt who left a gift on a table next to her. On her right was her mother-in-law and on her left her mother. Just then, she noticed Rahel, standing in the doorway. Their eyes met. They each smiled a frightened smile at the other and then Rahel disappeared. The light seemed to dim with her absence. Rebecca heard the children playing in the courtyard. She had a sudden urge to rush out the door and play with them, but she was stuck here in the room sitting modestly with the women. WOMEN! She suddenly realized she really was a woman. In her ear was a buzzing and Rebecca realized that the room was full of women chatting about her, marriage, and men.

"Rebecca, my dear, remember your husband is your master, but you are his pearl," one ancient aunt said to her.

A cousin whispered in her ear, "Without you, he is not complete."

And then that cousin's sister whispered in the other ear, "neither are you complete without him."

Some of Rebecca's cousins, one of whom was quite pregnant, were gathered in a corner of the room, looking at her knowingly, and giggling. She did not know what they were being so secretive about. She felt oddly out of place. What great knowledge did they have that she didn't?

The day wore on, and toward evening Jacob appeared in the doorway. "Mother. Rebecca. It is time to leave."

Jacob's sisters crowded around Miriam and Rebecca, each vying for the privilege of helping their mother stand and properly wrap her peçe. Then the sisters ushered Miriam, Rebecca, and Jacob toward the door in such haste that Rebecca barely had a chance to grab her mother's hand.

Jacob lingered on the threshold only long enough to make sure that his mother and his betrothed were beside him. Then he proudly turned and strode toward the exit, passing through the encroaching well-wishers like Moses parting the Red Sea. Rebecca was swept along with the crowd. She was overwhelmed with fear and excitement.

Rahel stood at the back of the room, her eyes filling with tears. She did not want to see Rebecca go. She did not have a chance to kiss her goodbye.

Miguel and David stood together, jostled by the energetic crowd.

Miguel rubbed his head in confusion. "Where are they going?" he asked with concern.

"They are leaving," responded David airily. Now that the event had taken place, he decided to accept all that went with it. There was no point in protesting since his concerns were not going to be taken into account.

"Yes, I see that. But why is Rebecca leaving with Jacob?" Miguel demanded, his voice rising in agitation.

David looked at him, confused by the question. "Miguel, they are betrothed. Rebecca will now live with Jacob."

Chapter 19

"And the wedding ceremony?" Miguel asked, eyes wide in amazement.

"The wedding ceremony will be soon enough, in a year. Sooner if Rebecca gets pregnant."

Miguel paused a moment to absorb this information. He tried to control his shock and dismay. His voice shaking in anger, he said, "How can you allow your own sister to live with that man without the benefit of marriage? It is against God's law."

"What do you mean?" David replied, his voice rising. "That is our practice! It is God's law."

"It is a disgusting practice!" Miguel exploded. "It is against God! It is against Judaism!"

The children stopped playing and stared at the two young men. A prickly silence fell over the crowd. The men watched, aghast.

David was now furious. "How can you say that to me?!" he shouted. "In my father's house! In the middle of my sister's kiddushin! This is the way it has always been done in our community. There is nothing wrong with our traditions. You have no right to comment on how to practice Judaism. Our ways are ancient. Certainly older and more respected than those of Marranos," David retorted spitefully.

Shaking with anger, Miguel leaned close to David's face. "I cannot stay here another moment," he said through clenched teeth. He turned, and pushed his way through the crowd, bumping into people right and left. Shivering with rage and humiliation, he stormed out of the house.

David stood frozen, his face flushed, too stunned to move. The skin on the back of his neck and on his cheeks felt hot and prickly. A long, uncomfortable silence followed Miguel's departure. Finally, Hayyim made his way to the center of the crowd.

"My friends," he bellowed. "This is a celebration! Eat! Drink! Enjoy yourselves, please." Slowly, the men returned to their conversations, the children to their games. David crept out of the room and into the garden. Rahel was staring at him, her eyes wide. David pushed past her, anger and shame already waging a battle within him.

Miguel walked briskly, winding his way through the streets without realizing where he was going. Soon, he found himself at the port. He picked up a rock and threw it, watching the little ripple it made as it sank. Hours passed, and he sat at the port, throwing rocks and watching seagulls career on the wind in the sunset. As his anger dissipated, it was replaced with feelings of confusion and humiliation. He knew it was not his place to criticize his host at a family event. Why had he done it? Was he really disgusted?

He realized that he was just as afraid as David had been. One day, someone would marry Clara and she would leave their little family to live elsewhere. But unlike Rebecca, Clara would stay in their home until her wedding day. She would be safe and protected. He feared Clara's leaving. She was all he had left of his parents. He barely remembered them, but believed it was their wish that he take care of her. No matter that Tía Maria and Abuela had been there, looking out for them and keeping them together. He had always taken extra care of Clara. Still, he knew that she needed to get married, have children, and find the other part of herself in a husband. He knew that he would do the same when he found a wife.

Questions tumbled in his mind. David was his only friend. Why had he been so rude to him? He had insulted David and his entire family, and the entire community. "What will I do now?" Miguel thought, miserably. Surely, Señor Hayyim had heard his fight with David, and so had the entire community. Maybe he should get on the next boat and leave. Disappear forever into the vast world. But that would break his grandmother's heart, and he could never leave his sister. That was no real solution. He would most certainly be without a job. How would the Vide family survive without his earnings?

Miguel looked up and realized that it was nearly dark. It was past time to go to evening prayers. How would he ever face his congregation? It never took long for news to travel in the Jewish community—even when passing from one ethnic group to another. With a heavy heart, he arose and headed slowly back to the Jewish quarter and evening prayers.

Chapter
20

Miguel arrived at the synagogue near the end of the evening service. The room was crowded so he stood by the door. He participated only half-heartedly. He was preoccupied with how badly he had behaved and how disappointed everyone would be in him. When the service ended, Miguel waited near the gate for José.

José greeted him with a grin, "How was the kiddushin?" he asked. Taking a look at Miguel's face, he asked. "But why do you look so dejected?"

Apparently, the news had not yet reached him.

With a sigh, Miguel fell in step with José and they started to walk home. As they walked, Miguel tried to explain what had happened. Yet every time he opened his mouth, all he could do was gasp—like a fish out of water.

They walked a long, circuitous path home until finally Miguel was able to speak. He described the argument with David, the terrible things he had said. "I do not know why I did this," he exclaimed. "I do not know how it happened, but I told David that his Judaism is wrong and stupid and ungodly. Oh José," he cried, "What am I going to do? What are we all going to do? I'm sure that Señor Hayyim will fire me. No one else will hire me now. No Romaniote will want such a mean-spirited person in his or her business and no Spaniard will want someone whom the Romaniotes hate. I've lost my best friend. Maybe I should run away."

José was silent. They walked together, footsteps echoing in the emptying streets.

By this time they had arrived at home, but neither wanted to go in, so they stood in the doorway. José was unsure of what to say. Whereas Miguel spoke freely, José used words sparingly. He knew he would never have created such a situation, but was not surprised that Miguel had done so.

Finally, as dusk was settling around them, José spoke. "You have done a disastrous thing, Miguel. Your actions will reflect upon the entire Sephardic community." He grabbed Miguel by the arm, afraid he would try to run. "We must speak to Abuela about this." Without releasing Miguel's arm, José steered him inside.

They were greeted by a warm scene that almost made Miguel cry. Teresa was setting the table, Maria was finishing the harissa of wheat and chicken by mashing them together, and Clara sat at her table sculpting a swan from marzipan. How could he have done it? They depended upon him to support them and to uphold the family honor. Heavily, the two men sat at the table.

"Abuela," began José, "we have a matter of great importance to discuss and we need your wisdom." Teresa heard the severity in José's tone and sat down, holding a pile of plates in her lap. While she was pleased to be considered wise and worthy of consultation, this request indicated a serious problem that was much more than a boys' squabble. José turned to Miguel and so did Teresa.

They waited. The room was silent.

Maria and Clara continued working because they could not stop without ruining their food. Besides, they did not want to appear to be eavesdropping. The silence got thicker and the room grew darker. Maria lit some oil lamps. A few times Miguel seemed to be ready to speak. He would draw a deep breath and open his mouth. Then he closed it again. No one moved.

Finally, Miguel drew a deep breath, looked his grandmother in the eye, and dropped his head to look in his lap where his hands lay twisting. He began: "Abuela, at the kiddushin I saw something horrible. So contrary to everything Jewish that I have learned that I had to speak out and in doing so I insulted David and his family. I have disgraced us all—the entire community. I'm sure I've lost my job. I believe I should go away."

Teresa thought for a moment. "What was so terrible that happened?"

Miguel raised his eyes to look at his grandmother, but his head stayed down. "After the kiddushin and the party, Rebecca left her father's house with Jacob and his mother—to his home—to be his wife! Without ever standing together under the huppah! No wedding ceremony. Just a betrothal, and that is all!"

Maria was unable to contain herself. "These Jews have no respect for women. Their girls are not only married as near children, but they are given to the groom before the wedding. What of honor and respectability?"

"Hush, daughter," hissed Teresa. "Miguel, you spoke because you felt strongly and that is wonderful. It is good because you have convictions you feel you must defend. And it is good because we are in a place where it is safe enough for you to do so. Your parents would be proud of you." Miguel smiled a shy smile. Teresa's face grew serious. "But you chose a bad time. You are right—we are all disgraced. If you flee, the burden of that disgrace will not only follow you, it will remain here with us. Not only will it hang over this family and keep José and Clara from marrying, but it will cloud the future of all Sephardim in Thessaloniki." She paused. "You must ask forgiveness of men, Miguel, before you can ask forgiveness of God. That is what we are reminded of on Yom Kippur. You must make this right."

"But, Abuela," Miguel stammered, his face now level with hers. "How can I do that? David was more than my friend—he was my defender."

Teresa took a deep breath, "Miguel you must go and ask their forgiveness. Whatever we may think of their customs, they are their customs. We are guests in this community. We could lose our livelihoods. They could petition the sultan to send us away, and we would need to find another ruler to invite us in. For the well-being not only of yourself, but of the entire community, you must go!"

"But Abuela," cried Miguel, "what will I say? What will I do?"

Teresa looked as though she was going to cry. "I cannot tell you. According to Jewish custom, the apology must be sincere. You must figure it out. But you must do it."

She stood slowly, and turned to Maria and Clara. "Come, Maria, it is time for supper."

Teresa laid the plates out on the table, and the other two women served the meal. The meal was a silent affair. No one dared talk or look at Miguel. In fact, no one looked up from his or her food. Miguel barely touched his dinner; the pain of his disgrace overshadowed his hunger. No one came to visit that evening. It did not take long for the community to learn of Miguel's outburst. Everyone was waiting for Miguel to save the community he had just destroyed. Until he did, they felt that they had to ostracize him and his family as well. After the meal, José tutored Clara in the Hebrew prayers. Then they all went to bed early, feeling this expulsion from the Sephardic community far more than they ever did the exile from Spain.

Miguel could not sleep. He tossed and turned, until finally he got up and quietly left the room to wander the streets of the neighborhood searching for a way to make his peace with David. Miguel did not go home in the morning. He had walked every street in the Jewish neighborhoods at least twice and then retraced his earlier path down to the wharf. There, he watched the sun rise over the sea. There, he said his morning prayers and then made his way to Hayyim's house.

Chapter
21

After Miguel had stormed out of Hayyim's house, David went and hid on the roof. As soon as he could excuse himself, Hayyim came to see what the matter was. He had seen Miguel rush off, and had heard the shouts exchanged between the boys, but he had not heard the argument himself. And since rumors were beginning to circulate already, he wanted to make sure he learned the truth.

Before Hayyim even stepped through the doorway, David turned his red face to him and snarled, "You're here to gloat! Yes, you were right. This was not the event to invite Miguel to. I'm sorry I ruined the party. I'm sorry I've embarrassed you in front of Jacob. I learned my lesson. I'll never invite Miguel or any of his kind around again." With that he threw himself face down on the roof, his head in his arms.

Hayyim was distressed by his son's words and behavior. As much as he felt uncomfortable with this display of emotion, he disliked the quick turn David had done on his friend. He liked Miguel. The boy was kind, considerate, smart, and loyal. Miguel had proven himself to Hayyim. He was the sort of friend that Hayyim wanted his sons to have—that he was Sephardic was of concern, but less so than in the past.

"David, you must mind how you speak to your father," Hayyim said sternly. And then, more softly, he asked, "What has happened? What have you done to embarrass me?"

"I am sorry, Father. But do you mean that no one has told you?" David sobbed in disbelief, his voice muffled by his arms. "Miguel almost tried to stop Rebecca from going home with Jacob. He said that it was ungodly to allow them to live together, that our traditions are disgusting! How could he say such a thing?"

Hayyim sat down next to David and rested his hand on his son's back. He was stunned. There were many situations that he might have envisioned, but never had he expected such an outburst from Miguel. Now, he too was angry. But his anger would not cure the problem. This event would create much tension among the Jews. There would be feuds and the Muslim rulers would not understand and would tax the Jews as a whole for any interruptions to the town's business. He realized that if he could get the boys back together, then the first step in healing the Jewish community as a whole would take place.

Hayyim measured his words carefully. "We must remember that our culture is different from theirs. Yes, we are all Jews, but they are learning how to live as Jews in freedom. So we must be patient." David looked at him quizzically. "No, David, Miguel was not right in making such a comment, especially at the party, but he needs to learn our customs. You may not be aware, but the Ashekanzim too will not let their daughters live with the groom until they have been wed under the huppah. It is a different interpretation of the law."

"Father," David sobbed, "I have lost a good friend. I cannot go to him. He has shamed us."

"In that you are right," replied Hayyim. "You have lost a good friend and this is not something for which you can apologize. But you can leave opportunities for him to come to you and you can be gracious and understanding should he ask for forgiveness. You worry about Miguel, and I will worry about how to appease Jacob and the community. Now, you must come out and see the guests." With that Hayyim patted David on the back and left him. Hayyim did not return to the party with a light heart, but his guests never knew. Eventually, David did come out and join the party, but his sadness and anger were easy for others to see. In fact, David was not sure which emotion was the stronger: anger at Miguel's outburst, or sadness at the loss of his friend.

Later that evening, after most of the guests had departed, Hadassah left her sisters and Dinah cleaning in the kitchen and hurried to find Hayyim. She discovered him pacing in the corridor, hands clasped behind his back.

"What has happened?" she asked. "I heard Miguel and David arguing. The children came running in frightened. They said Miguel left early. Why is David still upset?"

Hayyim was always amazed at how Hadassah knew everything, even when she was hidden away with the other women.

"Hadassah, Miguel is having some difficulties adjusting to our customs," Hayyim explained to his wife simply. It would do no good to tell her the whole story. If he did, she would never forgive Miguel. She was a stubborn woman who defended her family even if they were wrong. Without support, Miguel and David would never be able to mend their friendship. "Better to let the boys work it out," Hayyim said.

Hadassah was not a simple-minded woman. She realized that Hayyim's answer was an over simplification. Still, she knew her husband well enough to understand that no more information would come from him, and so she went in search of David. He was pacing the courtyard. His emotions were overpowering and he could not keep still. Hadassah walked in and sat on the bench where she had spoken about her dreams to her daughters. She patted the seat and invited him to sit with her. David gave his mother a nasty look and continued pacing and staring up at the sky.

"My son," began Hadassah, choosing to ignore the look, "what has upset you so that you cannot sit and chat with your mother?"

"Mother, I cannot discuss this with you," was David's strained reply. "This is a matter between Miguel and me. It is a matter of honor and law. Nothing that a woman should worry about. Nothing that a mother can help with. Go away! Leave me alone!" With that outburst, David began kicking rocks and fruit pits around the courtyard. Why had he spoken to his mother that way? She was always supportive of him and patient with his questions. Now he was even angrier with himself for adding disrespect to his mother to his list of grievances. Hadassah paused and opened her mouth to reprimand her son. But, being a wise woman, she realized anything she said would only be responded to with anger. So she rose majestically from the bench, angrily turned around, and stalked back to the kitchen.

It did not take long for David's nervous energy to force him outside the house to wander the streets.

When David returned home near midnight, there was a lamp lit in the formal room. There his father sat, awake, straight as a rod with his mother asleep, her head resting on his father's shoulder. Quietly, he came into the room. The flame in the lamp quivered.

Hayyim stared straight at David and asked in a loud whisper, "Where have you been? Your mother has been sick with worry!"

"I went to the square and sat. I prayed. I thought," responded a rather subdued David.

Hadassah twitched and now half awake cried out, "Hayyim! There is the ghost of David. Oh Lord! Why did not God take me instead?!"

"Hush, my wife," soothed Hayyim. "That is not a ghost. That truly is David. He only went for a walk. Come. Let us go to bed." With an angry and disgusted look at David, Hayyim took his wife and the lamp and went to bed. David was left behind in the dark room alone.

Chapter

22

As always, Dinah was the first awake in Hayyim's house. Once she washed and dressed, set out fresh washing water for the family, and lit the fire in the kitchen to start breakfast, she went into the formal room to begin tidying. She did not know that Rahel had cleaned it twice the day before. There she found David, asleep on some cushions, clutching a small pillow. She leaned over and tried to wake him. Slowly, he came back to the reality of the day. As he did so, Dinah went about her tasks in the rest of the house. It concerned her greatly that David had spent the night sleeping somewhere other than his bed, but at least it was in the house. However, since it was not her place to scold him and since he had not done damage to anything, she could not say anything.

Hayyim awoke, washed his face and dressed, then found David in the formal room. Mordechai, well slept, entered the room and gloated. He had known Miguel to be a problem and now it was proven.

Normally, the three of them would go to the synagogue for morning prayers; this morning, however, they silently put on their tefillin and tallitot and prayed quietly on their own. Once they finished, they joined the women in the courtyard for breakfast.

The mood was subdued, more than should have been the day after a kiddushin. No one quite knew what to say. Each was lost in thought. Not a word was spoken except for the Motzi and then the blessing at the end of meal.

When they had finished, Hayyim stood up and said, as he did every morning when he went to the store, "My wife, may your day be filled with sunshine." Then he stopped because his next line had to be changed. Everyone noticed his pause. "Kookla listen carefully to your mother, she is filled with wisdom. And Rachamim, you little rascal, behave." He smiled a gentle smile at his family. "Come my sons. It is time to find the perfect homes for our precious guests." David smiled a crooked smile at the familiar phrase. Then Hayyim left without even checking to see if Mordechai and David were with him. They followed.

David was nervous. "Would Miguel be at work today?" he wondered.

Mordechai stood tall beside his father, his face aglow. "Now everyone will know how troublesome these Sephardim are," he thought. "Maybe the sultan will throw them out so real Jews can live in peace."

Hayyim was worried about David and about Miguel. They arrived at the store and unlocked it. All day David was distracted. He kept looking at the door waiting for Miguel to arrive; then he remembered he was angry with Miguel. The day was a muddle of emotions.

Hayyim watched his younger son carefully, in between helping customers. The news had traveled and as the customers arrived they each wished Hayyim's family well on their celebration and offered some comment, mostly criticism, on Miguel's behavior. Occasionally, a long discussion would arise, which Hayyim tried to squelch and Mordechai encouraged, concerning the rising foreign population in the Jewish quarter and what was to be done about it.

During the afternoon, Juan stopped in. He was uncomfortable and had worried all morning about going to Hayyim's to inquire about his fabric. He had heard the talk around town about the spat between his friend Miguel Vide and David bar Hayyim. Finally, over lunch Eva had told him to stop agonizing and take action. So there he stood in the store.

Juan looked around. Hayyim was busy with a pair of Muslim men who were buying some expensive blue cloth with silver shot running through it. Mordechai was reshelving some bolts that had been left out. He turned, saw Juan standing hesitantly in the doorway and coldly returned to his work. Juan knew that Hayyim's older son had seen him and purposely ignored him. This only made him more uncomfortable.

David was nowhere to be seen. Finally, the two Muslims passed him at the door. He waited.

Hayyim called over to Mordechai, "Go and see what Kyrio Juan wants."

Mordechai ignored the request, and buried himself in the shelves of fabrics.

Hayyim felt his anger rising, but walked calmly over to Juan Abravanel. "What can I do for you?" he inquired casually, in Greek.

Juan answered in Ladino. "What has happened to my cloth? Have you sold it?"

"I am sorry. I do not understand," Hayyim returned. He felt sorry for this man trying to make a life in a land foreign to him with a language he did not understand. At the same time, this inability to communicate kept him from having to explain that none of Juan's fine fabric had been sold. From the shadowy corner where Mordechai was working, Hayyim heard a snicker. Juan looked around desperately for David to translate. When he realized his young friend was not there, he turned dejectedly to the door. "Shalom," called Hayyim with a false cheery note. Juan did not respond as he left.

When his shadow had passed from the door, Hayyim turned to Mordechai. "Your behavior was despicable. I will not have my employees, worse yet my sons, treat anyone, no matter who he or she, with such disrespect!" he roared. "And when I tell you to look after a customer, you will do as I say. I do not wish to hear from you again today."

Mordechai opened his mouth to speak, but realized, as he looked at his father's face, that to speak would only make the matter worse. He was not pleased at being reprimanded for his actions against those whom he viewed as usurpers, but he dutifully returned to his work.

Hayyim returned to his own work trying to hide the dissatisfaction he felt with himself. There was more he could have done for Juan. He could have made more of an effort to sell the cloth. He could have sent Mordechai to find David to act as translator. Mordechai, he was sure, knew Spanish by now. Mordechai was so good at learning languages, but he refused to admit to having learned Spanish. But there was something inside Hayyim that refused to offer more than basic courtesy to this stranger.

When the day was over, they finished their routine and left the store.

As Hayyim was locking the door, David asked in a quiet voice, "Do you think Miguel will come back?"

Mordechai quickly responded with, "Only long enough to be fired. We certainly do not want someone with his uncouth and uneducated ways."

David retorted, "He is well educated, just not about Jewish things."

"Well, that was obvious yesterday," hissed Mordechai. "None of my friends would be so crude as to insult my customs."

"None of your friends is from outside our family," responded David, raising his voice. "Besides, he did not know. Miguel just does not understand. Yes, he should have been more polite, but you are being ... a boor!" David was now screaming as they stood in the middle of the street.

"Hush, my sons," insisted Hayyim. "This is no place for a discussion such as this. Let us go home and talk in a civilized fashion." Hayyim looked around at the others staring at his sons.

"Very well," the younger men said in unison, and sullenly they marched home. Hayyim followed them desperately trying to think of a way to resolve this conflict.

The moment the brothers entered their home they started again.

"I do not understand how you can defend Miguel," began Mordechai. "He embarrassed himself by criticizing our customs. What does he even know of Jewish customs?"

"He does not know and so we should teach him," was David's quick reply. His mind was racing—why was he defending Miguel? But there was no way he would let Mordechai know his doubts. "I'm angry at him, but I can still understand why he said what he did."

By this time, Hadassah had rushed from the kitchen at the back of the courtyard to see what the fuss was. Usually, their home was a quiet one. There were her older two sons near the entrance so enraged they were ready to have a fistfight. Her first thought was to get between them, like she had when they were little. Hayyim rushed in from the street—he had heard the shouting as well. His feraçe billowed behind him.

He sternly called out, "Hadassah," and that stopped her in her tracks. Almost never did he command her to do anything, so when he did actually invoke his power as her husband she followed. Instead she rushed to be with her husband. Together, they stood aside. This was one time when they could not resolve the problem between their sons.

Mordechai's rage reached a boiling point, "You brought him to our business and our home. You shamed us at Rebecca's kiddushin. You are as much to blame as he. You are shameful!"

Hadassah gasped in shock and yelled out unable to contain herself anymore, "How dare you! No one in this family is shameful." Mordechai, David, and Hayyim looked at her in shock; they had never heard her raise her voice in such a way. She continued without a breath, without noticing their reaction, "No one is shameful in our kehillah. Have I taught you anything? Is this how I raised you? You bring shame on me to suggest such a thing." With that she stormed back to the kitchen.

Mordechai hung his head. The entire family had a deep respect for Hadassah. For the moment, the fight had lost its punch. David took this opportunity to escape the family to his hiding place on the roof.

Chapter
23

After his lonely morning prayers, Miguel contemplated what to do for the day. He certainly could not go to work. He could not face his friend David, or David's father and brother. In fact, he did not want to see anyone. Even his morning hunger was not enough to make him go home. Stymied by his sadness and moral struggle, Miguel spent the whole morning sitting in the same spot. The sailors ignored him as they did everyone else who did not interact with them. After all, many people came to the docks to watch them work and to dream of going off to exotic places.

At his home over breakfast, there was much anxiety.

"Where has he gone?" asked Teresa. "José, you'll have to go find him."

Clara chimed in with a wail, "What will we do if he is gone?"

"What a terrible thought, child," was Maria's horrified reply. "Do not dare repeat it."

"Abuela," replied a mournful José. "I cannot go. I must work at the silversmith's."

"Go and ask for the day off to find Miguel," Teresa commanded. "He is your cousin. He is our charge; he is our family. You must find him!"

José knew there was nothing else he could do but what his grandmother expected.

He went to the silversmith for whom he worked and asked permission to find his missing cousin, "Señor, I ask for today only to hunt the city to find my cousin."

"Ah, your cousin is the one who told the truth to the Grecos," said the silversmith. "I like honest men. When you find him tell him I'll find him a job. I do not see what the uproar is about anyway. After all, how many Grecos are there? Not enough to be counted after us. They will come round, if only because we out number them …." He would have continued if José had not dashed away. Right now José's only concern was his cousin.

José did not even know where to begin looking. He wandered up one street and down the next. After two hours, he realized that he had covered almost the entire Jewish quarter and not found him.

He leaned against a wall and thought, "Where? Where would you go, little cousin?" A seagull flew overhead, screaming. José looked up and said a prayer of thanks, "Of course, the wharf! We used to love sitting on the deck of a ship watching the gulls."

Off he dashed through streets, his open feraçe blowing behind him. He ran around the vendors carrying trays of food and the porters lugging huge bundles on their backs. Once he had to stop to avoid a number of Muslim officials who were taking notes as they strolled past stores. Finally, he saw the ships in the docks.

"Please, oh please, let him be here," José quickly surveyed the scene. A ship was just departing. José's heart broke. "NO," he cried in his head, "please do not let our Miguel be on that ship." He strained to see his cousin on the deck. He could not tell. He looked down the dock on his left and then his right. Wait! There was a figure all the way at the point. Could it be?

José ran in the hot midday sun to the end of the pier. There sat Miguel staring out to sea.

José stopped beside him, breathing hard. Miguel did not turn to look at him. For a long while neither spoke. They sat next to each other watching the waves crash at their feet and the gulls fly overhead.

After what seemed an eternity, José said very quietly, "We missed you at breakfast."

"Sorry," mumbled Miguel.

Chapter 23

"Where were you this morning?" asked José.

"Who knows," was the response.

"What are you going to do?"

"Not sure."

"Abuela told you what to do."

"Apparently, she told you as well," chided Miguel. They never turned their heads, but their eyes met and they broke out in big smiles. "She is good at that you know."

José responded with a grin, "I know, I'm here." Again they lapsed into silence. They stayed that way for a long time.

As evening came upon them, they heard the imams calling the Muslims to come for evening prayer.

José once again broke the silence, "It is almost time for our evening prayers as well."

Miguel was as sullen as before, "I know."

"Shall we go then?" asked José, trying to be casual.

"Why should I?" questioned Miguel.

José took a deep breath; he realized this was not going to be easy, "Because it is time. Is there any more to say? And," here he tried to bring back his cousin's smile, "because if I do not come home with you, then Abuela will banish me."

Miguel sat for one moment more looking out into the vastness of the sea and then turned and looked at José. José saw great pain in his dear cousin's face.

"The last thing I want is to disappoint Abuela," Miguel replied slowly. The two rose from their places, stretched for a moment, and turned back to the town that was now their home. Then they slowly made their way to the warmth of their kahal.

The nearer they got to the synagogue, the slower Miguel walked; he dreaded every step. Sensing his fear, José put a protective arm around the younger man.

Without looking at José, Miguel asked, "What are people saying?"

"I'm not sure," replied José, "since I spent the day with you. However, what I have heard is that some of our people believe you committed a grave error." With that Miguel's shoulders slumped. "But some are praising you for stepping forward and speaking your mind." And José felt Miguel stand taller. "Still others do not think it really matters because there are not enough Grecos—pardon me—Romaniotes to matter." At this, Miguel paused in his steps, and then José whispered in his ear, "I have heard a rumor that at the Kal de los Locos—the Congregation of the Crazies ... okay the Ashkenazim—they want to make you a saint." This made Miguel snigger, and so the two continued down the street.

When they finally arrived at the door to the synagogue, the crowd chatting outside grew quiet. The Sephardim looked at Miguel doubtfully and he returned each stare. They wanted to see what kind of man was standing before them; he wanted to see how they felt about him. At first, he looked back with fear or resentment, but slowly his confidence grew until he felt courage by simply confronting these men. The crowd closed around José and Miguel and they entered the building for evening prayers.

When the prayers were over, they left the synagogue. José's arm was still draped across his cousin's shoulder.

He whispered, "What shall we do now?"

Miguel stopped in his step. Had his cousin said "we?"

He turned with a grin, looked José square in the face, and said, "We will go home for dinner. I'm starved." Then he put his arm around his cousin's waist and together they headed home.

Chapter
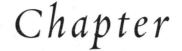
24

The cousins arrived home at their usual time. No comment was made during dinner about Miguel's disappearance. The conversation centered around other community gossip.

When the meal was over, Teresa turned to Clara, "I think you ought to go to the public well and refill our urn."

Clara looked at her in surprise.

"But Abuela, I go every morning. We should have enough water until then."

Maria rose from her chair. She knew Teresa's intent, "Child, how many times must I remind you not to argue with your Abuela. Come, I will go with you." And with that she reached for her feraçe.

Clara realized two things at that moment. The first was that she was going to the well to get water they probably did not need, and the second was that Abuela wanted her out of the house. She studied her brother as she wrapped herself in her feraçe and reached for the urn. What did her grandmother intend to do with him? All day, Abuela had been distracted but gentle. They had all been distracted wondering where Miguel and José were. Ever since they had left Spain, all major decisions, and even most minor ones, were made together. There was nothing to do, however, but go. Her aunt was busy rushing her out the door.

Once Maria and Clara were gone, Teresa turned her now serious face to Miguel, "There is no excuse for disappearing the way you did. Your aunt and I have lost enough; we deserve to know where you are."

"I was not thinking," was Miguel's immediate reply. "Or maybe I was thinking too much." That brought a nervous giggle from José.

Teresa glared at José and returned her attention to Miguel, "Since you've thought so much, what have you been thinking about?" Then she sat back and folded her hands in her lap in expectation.

Miguel took a long, slow breath. He had been expecting this conversation. But he was not prepared for how difficult it would be. "I was trying to decide how to approach David," he began. "I still believe what they do is wrong … but I also know I stated my beliefs in the wrong way at the wrong time." Teresa nodded her approval. "I know that I must apologize. The question is how. I must maintain my dignity and my beliefs, without belittling David and his people's."

José interrupted, "Does this all really matter? There are plenty of jobs now among us. We do not have to have anything to do with the Grecos if we do not want to."

Teresa looked at her eldest grandson in horror. "Whether you choose to spend time with the Romaniotes is your business, but to insult people is not the proper way to behave. I did not raise you to behave in such a manner. I am disappointed with your attitude." Then she purposely turned her chair so that her back would be toward him.

Taking Miguel's hand in hers, she spoke to him gently. "Miguel, my dear, your pondering has done you good. You have reached a serious juncture; an adult moment that even most adults do not approach appropriately. I am not sure there is much guidance I can offer. However, I am here to listen."

As soon as they stepped from the house, Clara burst out, "Tía Maria, what is Abuela saying to Miguel?"

"Really, child, what makes you say Abuela is doing or saying anything out of the ordinary?" asked Maria, just as anxious about what was going on between her mother-in-law and nephew.

"Tía Maria, I'm not stupid. I'm not a little girl. We both know that we do not need water until the morning," Clara responded a bit annoyed. "Abuela is not going to do anything terrible to Miguel, is she?"

Chapter 24

"Clara," Maria said gently as she put her hand on the girl's face, "your grandmother would not do anything terrible to any of you. You three are our lives, our future, we have sacrificed everything for you. She is going to help him all she can."

Clara was not sure that answer would satisfy her, but she realized that her aunt did not know much more than she did. They walked in silence down the street until they reached the corner where the well stood. A small crowd of women was gathered there. Bringing water to the home was women's work and only those who owned an entire house, which was rare, would have a private well. Almost everyone used some kind of public well. The crowd grew silent as Maria and her niece approached. Maria took a deep breath and stood up tall and straight. She was not sure what these women were going to say, but she was sure it would be about Miguel.

One woman could barely wait until the two were in earshot and called out, "Has your wandering son returned home?"

Maria gripped Clara's arm to keep her quiet and responded only when they were close enough that she could do so in a normal voice, "Do you mean my nephew? He never went wandering without us." With this comment, smiles spread throughout the group of Sephardic women. The woman who had asked the question was known by all to be a trouble maker. With a toss of her head, she picked up her urn and left the group. Maria smiled to herself.

One of their friendlier neighbors asked more gently, "Has Miguel come home? My husband passed José in the streets looking desperately for him. We've all been worried. I do not know what I would do if one of my children went missing."

Maria looked at her kindly. Everyone knew that this family had lost their two oldest children to the Inquisition and had barely escaped with the other three.

"Yes, thank you. Miguel came home for supper. He was terribly hungry," was her reply.

"Where has he been?" asked a third neighbor. "Has he found another job? There is no point in going back to work for that Greco," she said, placing a negative emphasis on the last word. "There are plenty of Sephardim quite pleased with your boy for telling these backward Jews the truth about their bizarre customs. It is better if we remain with our own kind." Many of the women nodded in agreement with this last comment.

Clara jumped in innocently, "But are not all Jews of the same kind?" Many of these same women smiled at her just as they would a young child asking a simple question.

Maria gripped Clara's arm tighter, "Where my nephew decides to work is his business and mine, not yours. That is not the point. We must follow Jewish law."

"And what Jewish law must he follow here?" asked one women in total ignorance.

"That of respect. A guest does not embarrass his host. Nor does a Jew knowingly create a shame for the entire community." Maria's tone was haughty. As a Marrano she was quite proud of the Jewish knowledge she had acquired, even as the Inquisition closed in on her secret community.

Many of the women felt the sting of her remark and grew silent. A few even left for home feeling dismissed. Those who remained gave the two Vide women a wide berth. None wanted it to be known that they had insulted Teresa Vide's family. The Sephardic community had great respect for this matriarch. In silence, Maria and Clara filled their urn. Clara positioned it on her hip and imitated Maria's haughty demeanor as they retraced their steps. So it was that they returned proudly to a room filled with hushed tension.

Chapter
25

Miguel made the appearance of going to bed. Once he knew everyone was asleep, he lit an oil lamp and sat at the table. Something still concerned him that he had not discussed with his grandmother. He was not sure why, but he suspected his grandmother would not understand. David's friendship meant a great deal to him. He could not even explain it to himself. He sat through the night staring into the dim flame wondering what kind of relationship he would have with David after this was all over.

That, of course, brought his musings back to the mess he had created. He was deeply disturbed by the comments he had heard from people in his community. What right did they have to criticize the local Jews? The Romaniotes had been here much longer than the Sephardim. They had been steeped in Judaism for centuries. How much did most of the Sephardim know about Jewish custom? On the other hand, who gave the Romaniotes, Venetians, Provençals, or Ashkenazim any right to criticize his people when they could not even decide among themselves the proper way to be Jewish?

In the middle of the dark night, Maria awoke and saw her nephew deep in thought at the table. She was tempted to join him, but he seemed so involved in his own thoughts, and she thought it better if she left him alone to sort things out for himself. So she turned over and returned to the dreams of her lost husband and their home in Spain.

"What should I do?" was the question circling in Miguel's head. He knew he had to go to David's house and apologize to David and his family. What would he apologize for? His words? No, that he could not do. He believed in what he had said, a kiddushin is a kiddushin and a nisuin is a nisuin. One does not send a daughter away at the kiddushin, but at the nisuin. Then it must be for the timing of his words, or perhaps for the way in which they were spoken. Yes, that he could do. Without a doubt, he had spoken his feelings far too harshly and at an inopportune moment.

Miguel was so deep in contemplation, he did not realize that it was morning until everyone else started to get up and roll his or her mattresses for storage. A second night he had not slept. Yet this morning he felt better about himself and his situation. He knew that his family supported him. He knew what he had to do. The only two questions to answer were: when and how.

Chapter

26

W hile Miguel was being received warmly by his family and aided in his crisis, David ostracized himself from his. His family was torn in two over Miguel's outburst. Despite his mother's efforts, David refused to come down from the roof for dinner.

Hayyim brought it up for him, "Your mother does not think it proper for an old woman to climb on the roof so I brought you a plate of food."

"Thank you," his son grunted.

"You need not be surly with me," retorted his father. "I am distressed about this incident, as well. I am worried about Miguel, too."

"You are?" asked David with some relief. He had worried that his father would forbid their friendship.

"Of course I am. He is your friend. Is he not?"

David gave a half smile, "I think so. He was not very friendly at Rebecca's kiddushin."

"David, he was shocked by our customs. He is not used to anything we do. In a sense, he is not used to anything he does either," reminded Hayyim. "However, that does not mean I'm not disappointed with him and angry with him. He brought anger into our home during a celebration and that was inappropriate."

"How angry at him are you?" asked David rather concerned.

"What do you mean?"

"I guess...," here David paused thinking if he really ought to ask the question, "Does Miguel still have a job?"

"That is a serious question. I'm not sure," Hayyim replied honestly. "I cannot have someone in my store who causes dissention in my family. However, I also will not let prejudice guide my decision." David knew that this last comment was directed at his brother who had developed an intense hatred of the Sephardic community. "I guess we must wait and see what Miguel does before we can decide if he still has a job." David saw that this would be the best answer he would get from his father. "Now, my son, will you come down and join us for a quiet evening? Would you play a game of chess perhaps?"

Normally, David would have jumped at the offer of a game of chess. Usually, his father spent his evenings with Rachamim because he saw his other sons all day. Tonight, David was not interested.

"No thank you father, another time. I think for the moment I will stay up here. But thank you for the dinner."

Hayyim gave him a knowing smile and placed his right hand on his son's head, just as he did during his Sabbath blessing of his children. This act comforted both of them. Then he climbed back down to the courtyard. David could hear Rachamim and his father playing soldiers and a conversation between Rahel and Yaiya Rahel, their maternal grandmother, who was spending a few nights at their home following the kiddushin.

When the family went to bed, each called out his or her evening greeting to David on the roof. After they had gone, he came down, bringing his plate. First he took the plate to the kitchen, where Dinah was still cleaning up.

She looked up and smiled as he walked in. "Come Andropolaki, tell your Dinah what troubles you."

"Dinah, do you not know?" asked David, a bit annoyed. Only Dinah still called him by that pet name. It did not bother him anymore. To him she was an extra grandmother figure.

"Well, I know what my problems are, but what are yours?" she asked a bit coyly. While many thought because she was lame and hunched she was stupid, David had always respected her wisdom. He knew her to be gentle and protective, like a wolf mother, willing to give her life for the family that had taken her in. Often he had come to her, rather than to his own mother for protection from his older brother.

Chapter 26

Of course, by now, she had heard about the spat. Everyone, from the shopkeepers to the delivery boys, was talking about it.

David smiled at her and sat at the bench by the work table. She brought a bowl of pistachios and sat next to him. Her hump was so high, her face was slightly above table height. They sat in silence for a while cracking nuts. The pile of shells grew. She knew he would eventually talk.

Finally, he spoke, "Is Miguel really my friend?"

"Ah, the meat of the nut," responded Dinah. She smiled as she cracked another between her teeth. "What is a friend?"

David grinned. Dinah rarely answered his questions, but she gave him much insight into his problems. "I guess a friend is someone who sticks by you. Someone who is good to you. Someone who understands you." He stopped for a moment, "That would be you, would it not Dinah?"

Now she stopped and smiled at him. What did he know of her problems? He never listened to her heart. She loved him as she imagined she would have loved her own children; the children she would never have because no one would marry a hunchback lame girl with no dowry. Did David ever ask her how she felt about her own father who had sold her into slavery to save his other daughters from spinsterhood and his sons from the burden of caring for them? She let the thought pass and returned to David.

"Yes, little David, I am your friend. Who else do you count among your friends?"

"I would like to count Miguel. He has taught me so much about the world outside of Thessaloniki. Some day Father will send me out on one of the ships to travel and I know much more than I would otherwise." "And what have you given him, little man?" she asked as she rose to get another bowl full of nuts out of the barrel by the door.

"What have I given him? I do not know," was David's confused reply.

When Dinah finally settled herself, she turned to him and spoke, "You have given him a welcome here no else would have dared. You have accepted him as he is and shown him who you are. What else can friends do for each other? We must wait to see if he realizes that. Now, David, it is late. You need to go to bed as do I."

David rose from the table and kissed Dinah good night. While others might have considered the act unacceptable—a man kissing a woman who was not his wife, mother, or daughter—both knew the symbolism was simply one of a son kissing his mother. Then he left the kitchen and returned to the main house and his mattress. Dinah cleared away the nut shells, covered the embers in the fireplace with ashes to keep them warm until she arose in the morning, unrolled her mattress from the corner, and lay in front of the fire after removing much of her outer clothing. The entire house fell into the silence of night.

When Hayyim and Hadassah went to bed that evening, they had their usual discussion of events of the day. "Kookla, I'm terribly sorry about the boys' behavior," said Hayyim. "They really should not act like that. I'm not sure I understand why they are so at odds over this matter."

"My husband, you cannot control their emotions. They are brothers, and brothers will do battle over something all the time," Hadassah replied gently in the dark. "You cannot have them working together tomorrow. Maybe not for a long time, you know. Until some resolution is made, they will battle over Miguel. I wonder if hiring Miguel was the best thing to do."

Hayyim pondered this point as well for a while and then spoke into the darkness. "With the number of Sephardim in the town, it is necessary to be fluent in their language. By hiring him, the Sephardim know me to be a friend, and a friend of so many will surely make a profit. It is really not something to discuss, because what is done is done and cannot be undone." Hadassah thought on this point and made her agreement by reaching for her husband in the dark.

Chapter
27

The next morning began like any normal morning. David attended prayers with his father and brother at the Romaniote synagogue. There the community welcomed them as they had any other day. A number of congregants jokingly asked how the negotiations for peace between the Greeks and Spanish were going, but they received no response. Hayyim had told his sons not to engage in conversation that encouraged discussion of the incident.

When they arrived at the store, Hayyim announced, "David, I want you to make the deliveries today."

"I do not want to make deliveries," whined his younger son.

"They need to done and no one else is going to do them," responded his father rather sternly. Mordechai snickered. Hayyim spun on his heels and glared at his older son. "One more sound from you, and I'll have you making the deliveries today." Mordechai snapped into silence and scuttled to the back of the store to busy himself. Hayyim gathered a bundle of fabrics, "David, this bundle goes to the Muslim teacher's home at end of the road. Make sure to give it to the eldest woman slave. Apparently, the younger ones cut sections off before they give it to their mistress." David took the bundle and left the store without saying a word.

Not far away, in the Sephardic area of the Jewish quarter of Thessaloniki, José and Miguel also went to morning prayers at their synagogue. Miguel went with some trepidation because he really did not know how the community would act; besides he was totally exhausted. The men welcomed the Vides and made no comments. Since the community was divided over the argument, the general feeling was to leave it alone and see what happened.

After the morning prayers, they returned home for breakfast. Before he left for the silversmith's, José announced, "Abuela, Mother, I may be later than usual this evening. The silversmith may want me to work after prayers because I missed yesterday."

"Just send us word with our neighbor Señor Abravanel so we do not worry," his mother answered with a light tone. Then, José shut the door behind him. Miguel sat at the table unsure of what to do.

"Now Miguel," began his aunt, "what are your plans for this day?"

"I still cannot go to Señor Hayyim's store," he said, more to himself than her. "But there is no reason to be idle. Money must be earned." With that he rose and left the room without really answering his aunt's question.

Maria and Teresa looked at each other a bit concerned, "Mother-in-law, what did you say to that boy last night when you sent Clara out to the well?"

"My daughter, I told him that a man must be responsible for his actions. That was all," she retorted a bit defensively.

"So where has he gone for the day? You do know that he was up all night, again," commented the younger woman. Teresa was about to respond when Clara returned from washing the dishes in the courtyard trough. She came back energized from her chat with the other teenage girls and the opportunity to be independent.

When Miguel left home, he knew he had to do something physical. Despite his lack of sleep, the tension was building in his body and it needed to be released. He decided to visit some local merchants to see if they needed any deliveries made, so he began at a favorite green grocer in the farmer's market around the corner. This lonely man had made a good business buying from the local farmers and selling their produce in the market when they could not stay there all day, and he had no help. Miguel had learned that Señor Ferdinand Shoshan had left Spain with two small children, but they had not survived the boat ride. Many widows desired him for their husband; however, he had not answered any of them.

"Señor Shoshan, how have you been?" began Miguel. He hoped that he would not be engaged in a long conversation.

"Ah, my dear Señor Vide. I have missed you. Has your Tía released you yet, so that I can adopt you?" Ferdinand said this as more than a mere joke.

"No, Señor, I am sorry. Do you have any work for me today, perhaps?" asked Miguel.

Ferdinand thought for a moment. "I do indeed. Señora Botton always likes me to save her the best of whatever I have. Here is her bundle. Take it to her this morning and then she will not have to worry about when she can begin her supper. When you are done, come back."

Miguel was grateful for the job and the lack of commentary on his behavior. He took the bundle and headed to the Botton home. As he meandered, he thought. "There must be some way to approach David that would bring satisfaction to both of them." As he walked, he turned his head to look across the street. Miguel stopped in his tracks. There was David, carrying a bundle of fabrics. His initial reaction was to call out to his friend and tease him; David carried the bundle awkwardly. Then he stopped himself. They were not speaking any more. Sadly he looked away.

Just as he looked away, David turned around. Across the street was Miguel carrying a bundle.

"How easily he manages his load," thought David. He opened his mouth to yell to Miguel and then shut it abruptly. Miguel still had not apologized. Despite the great love that David had for his friend, he still felt very deeply the hurt that Miguel had caused his family.

Chapter
28

After a full day of deliveries, both David and Miguel were exhausted. They followed the same routine as usual. Each washed his face and arms at the place outside the synagogue set aside to do so and then entered for evening prayers. Afterward, they returned home for the evening meal. This evening David consented to eat with his family. He was too tired to argue with Mordechai, who believed that he had won his father's affection over David. In his eyes, David had been punished by being forced to act as an apprentice. The rest of the family remained relatively quiet, even Rachamim. After the parties and unrest, there was a welcome peace at the table. .

Later that night, in bed, Hadassah asked Hayyim, "How did the boys do today?"

Hayyim laughed, "How could they? Mordechai had to do all the work in the store and David was out all day. They both thought the deliveries were a punishment. At least that kept Mordechai quiet."

Hadassah also giggled, "How silly they can be. Just like children." This time Hayyim pulled Hadassah close to him and they fell asleep.

When Miguel and José arrived home after prayers, Clara immediately jumped on Miguel asking the question that had been on all the women's minds during they day, "Where were you all day? What did you do, Miguel?"

José waved her away, "Clara! Give us a chance to sit. Let your brother be."

"Your cousin is right, Clara," offered their grandmother. "It is not your business to ask such questions."

Clara marched over to the cook stove in a huff to get the soup. "Nothing is my business. I'm never allowed to ask anything. I hate being the littlest." Maria smiled tolerantly, but said nothing.

Teresa continued the conversation, however, "So do tell us Miguel how you spent your day." José looked at his brother apologetically. He could dismiss Clara simply using his age, but no one could dismiss their grandmother. Miguel shrugged his shoulders. "That is not an answer, young man," growled Teresa.

"Very well, I made deliveries for various people in the community." With that, he threw a few coins on the table and stormed out of the room.

"That did not go as well as you had hoped," Maria piped in sarcastically.

Teresa gave her a nasty look. José rose heavily to go after his cousin. "Sit down!" snapped Teresa. "There is nothing any of us can do except eat our supper." They did so in absolute silence. No one wanted to make Teresa any angrier.

Despite his hunger, Miguel could not bring himself to go inside. He stood outside the door for a few moments and then strode down the hall to their neighbor Juan Abravanel's home. There he paused for another moment before knocking.

Almost immediately Eva opened the door, her baby on her hip, "Señor Vide, what is the matter?"

"Why does anything have to be the matter for friends to visit friends?" asked Miguel as naturally as he could.

"Who is it?" called out Juan from inside the house.

"It is our neighbor, Señor Miguel Vide," responded his young wife.

Juan appeared suddenly at the door.

"Come in, come in. Have you eaten? We were just sitting down to dine." Miguel gladly took a seat. "What brings you to our humble home?" asked Juan with enthusiasm. He was a generous, hospitable man.

"I decided to stop at your home and see how you are," commented Miguel.

Chapter 28

Juan was not fooled. Rarely did people drop in during dinner time. But he was an understanding man. Should Miguel want to share his concerns about the disagreement, then he would.

"Wife," he called grandly, "bring an extra plate for our good friend." Eva smiled at Miguel sweetly as she deposited her baby in his father's lap and brought the food to the table. It was a simple meal of bread, cheese, and olives, but it was filling. During the meal there was simple chatter about the day and community gossip. When they had finished Eva took the dishes, her brother, and brother-in-law down to the courtyard, so that the men could chat. "Now Miguel," said Juan as he pushed his chair back from the table and bounced his baby on his knee, "what is it that I can do for you? Remember, it takes two to make an argument." Miguel smiled. Juan had a proverb for every occasion.

"I cannot stand being picked at. Every moment Abuela wants to know what I do, where I go. I cannot stand it any more!" He stood so swiftly his chair fell over, but he did not notice.

"Ah, problems happen in the best of families," commented Juan. "This will pass. It only feels like this until you stop noticing. What is really the problem?" Juan stood up. He picked up the fallen chair and put an arm around Miguel while holding the baby in the other. "I'm here to help you all I can. You are like family to me."

Miguel put his head face down on Juan's shoulder and wept, "I must go and apologize to David, and I do not know how."

Juan patted Miguel on the back, as he often did his young brother-in-law. He sighed.

After a few moments, he said, "I'm sorry. I cannot help you. I do not know. The only answer I have is that you must go and do so. However, I'm sure you will do it appropriately." Miguel dried his eyes on the back of his hand and looked at Juan, begging for more of an answer. Then he heaved a sigh and left the home that had offered him a moment of comfort. As he shut the door Juan said to no one in particular, "'May he have a smooth voyage.'"

Again Miguel went to the wharf and spent the evening there. When darkness fell, he made his way home knowing that his family would be getting ready for bed. In this way, he hoped he had avoided conversation. When he arrived, no one bothered him. No one spoke to him. In fact, they ignored him as if he was not there. When everyone was safely in bed, Maria blew out the one remaining lamp. Darkness fell. And again, Miguel was restless.

Chapter

29

Miguel got out of bed early. There was no point in staying in bed anymore. If he had slept, he did not remember and certainly did not feel like he had. After he got dressed, he neatly rolled up his mattress and crept out of the room. No one stirred. It was far too early.

Miguel slowly made his way through the Sephardic area of the Jewish quarter to the Romaniote one. He found David's house and knocked at the door. Dinah put down the urn of water she was carrying and went to answer the knock. There stood Miguel. Her first instinct was to shut the door and leave Miguel on the step. But she knew that that was not Hayyim's view of tzedakah—whoever knocked at the door was shown in and given basic hospitality. Still, she did not have to pretend to like providing the hospitality, so she contented herself with a cold stare and showed Miguel to the formal room. Slowly she went to awaken David. Why cause him to lose any more sleep than needed? After waking him, she ran to wake Hayyim and Hadassah.

Unceremoniously, she ran into their room, "Kyrio Hayyim, Kyria Hadassah, that Kyrio Miguel is here. David and he are alone in the formal room."

Hayyim and Hadassah sat bolt upright in their bed. They dressed quickly without their morning wash. Neither thought to reprimand Dinah for barging into the room. Then they ran to the formal room. Standing in the middle of the room was an unkempt, tired Miguel looking down at a bedraggled David, who was sitting uncomfortably on a stool. David had not even bothered to dress; he met Miguel in his bed clothes. Hayyim and Hadassah instinctively stopped outside the room and stood in the shadow of the doorway. They could not see directly into either boy's face.

The footsteps and banging doors awakened Mordechai. He, too, dressed, quickly washed his face and rinsed his mouth, and left his room to find out what had Dinah and his parents running around the house so early. He slipped up quietly behind his parents in the doorway. There, in the shadows, unseen by Hayyim, Hadassah, David, or Miguel, Mordechai watched.

David looked up at Miguel. His eyes could not focus on Miguel's face and reflected nothing. He was angry with himself, sad to lose Miguel, and tired; David was so overwhelmed by emotion, he felt nothing. He did not realize that he was clutching a pillow in his arms.

Miguel did not have David's benefit of a few hours of sleep. His face was gray and haggard. He knew that the burden of beginning the conversation was on him. While standing gave him the advantage of height, David's seated position gave him the advantage of power. Miguel knew that David's not inviting him to sit emphasized his unwelcome presence in the house. Miguel cleared his throat; he was hoarse from the tension, cold of night, lack of sleep, and thirst. Then he drew a deep breath. Feeling unready, but knowing he probably never would be ready, he began by choosing formality as a way to hide his nervousness.

"David, I am here at an early hour and I apologize to you and your family for disturbing your morning, but my business is important." David gave a grunt. Miguel paused, regained his courage, and continued, stuttering. "Your sister's kiddushin. It was an important day for her, your family, and the Jewish community. I was honored by your invitation to share in the joy."

"Were you really?" came David's sarcastic reply.

Hayyim was angered by David's callousness. Forgiveness was hard to request. And yet, he remained where he was. This argument was between the two young men, at least for the moment.

Miguel stopped. Should he answer this last remark? He decided not to, moving forward rather than backward seemed far more reasonable.

Chapter 29

"It is amazing to me to see Jews celebrate as Jews in public. It is hard to remember that there are different kinds of Jews and though we pray to the same God and follow the same laws, our customs are different. You are my first friend here, in my new home—my first friend who has never whispered in a corner in the dark in my ear half afraid 'I am a Jew. Are you?' You shout it to the world every day. And so, I have learned to shout as well. But I must learn you cannot shout everything, some things need to be discussed. Teach me, please. Help me learn when to shout in the sunshine, when to talk around the table, and when to whisper in the dark."

Hayyim and Hadassah stood in the doorway stunned. They looked at each other with the same thought in their minds: when did Miguel become so well spoken? Hayyim was impressed. Miguel had not only asked forgiveness, he had asked for help. David not only had to forgive, but would have to take on the role of teacher.

David's hands relaxed on the pillow. Did he really "shout" Judaism? Was it that simple?

David stood up and, in doing so, saw his parents. He smiled to them and raised an eyebrow. Haddasah grinned and dashed to the kitchen; something special had to appear for breakfast, not just because her son had forgiven his best friend, but because two divided communities would be united now. Mordechai was shocked. How easily his parents and brother accepted Miguel's apology. Could they be sure it was heartfelt?

David turned to Miguel, "Come. Father, Mordechai, and I have not yet said our morning prayers. Join us and then have breakfast with us."

The tension in Miguel's body disappeared in an instant. "But I must go to Jacob's house and ask his forgiveness. His family was greatly wronged by me."

Hayyim stepped forward and put a hand on Miguel's shoulder.

"There is no point in disturbing them this early. Pray with us, have breakfast with us, and then go. It is doubtful that my new son Jacob has arisen yet," he said with a small grin on his face.

"No," interrupted David, "have breakfast and then we'll both go."

With their arms around each other's shoulders and smiles on their faces, David and Miguel followed Hayyim into the courtyard. They knew that from now on, no conflict could divide them. They would use each other as a guide through the cloudy skies that would cast shadows on the Jewish community in the future.

Mordechai followed, as well. He could not object out loud to Miguel praying with them; that would be contrary to God's law. But he would watch Miguel. He believed Miguel would show his true non-Jewish self one day, and Mordechai would be there to point it out to his father and brother.

In the courtyard, drenched in sunshine, with no roof to block their voices rising up to God, Hayyim, Mordechai, David, and Miguel chanted their morning prayers and gave thanks for a new day.

Epilogue

Six months later, David and Miguel were again in the courtyard of David's synagogue. Both were in new clothes because they had grown significantly in the last half a year and because it was a very special occasion. Miguel felt particularly proud of his feraçe because it was new—no more rag merchant finds for his family. Kyrio Hayyim had given him a raise, José had found a partner and opened his own silver shop, and Clara's business was thriving.

Miguel stood proudly with his sister, cousin, and aunt at Rebecca's wedding. This time they had all been invited. David was with them as they watched the bride circle the groom seven times. Jacob stood still and grave under his tallit held up by two men.

David leaned in toward the family and explained, "Those two men are almost always the huppah bearers because they are so tall."

Maria nodded a thank-you. She was trying to make as many mental notes about the event as she could in order to inform her mother-in-law. Her children practically had to drag Maria to the wedding. She had wanted to stay home and nurse Teresa, whose health was failing.

Teresa, however, put on a cheery face and sent them off saying: "There's no reason for everyone to spend his or her whole day in this dreary room. We were invited and so we must go. Just go for me and tell me all about it, down to every detail." She had lain back on her pillows, rested the back of one forearm on her forehead and continued, "Besides, an old lady like me deserves a rest from your daily prattle. Go on! You'll be late!"

On their walk to the ceremony, José gave them a lecture on marriage customs he had learned from his business partner. "There are three stages to marriage, Avram explained to me: erusin, kiddushin, and nisuin. The erusin is when the couple is officially betrothed. Then there is the kiddushin, which is when the event is sanctified and this is when the seven blessings are recited. And finally is nisuin where the ketubbah is signed and read."

Here Clara interrupted, "What is a ketubbah?"

Maria turned to her niece and responded, "It is one of the things that sets Jews apart. It is a document given to a bride at her wedding and guarantees her rights as a wife."

"Apparently," continued José who had waited patiently for his mother to finish, "the difference between the Romaniote marriage ceremony and our tradition is when the kiddushin takes place. For us the kiddushin is tied to the nisuin; for the Romaniotes it is tied to the erusin."

Here Miguel jumped in, "But how could Rebecca have gone home with her fiancée?"

"Hush, Miguel!" commanded his aunt. "You do not need to speak so loudly." Miguel bit his lower lip in remorse.

José spoke more quietly now as they were entering the Romaniote section of the city. "You know there are other communities where the couple lives together and later their marriage is sanctified, like some peasants up north. Maybe like the crowns you saw at the kiddushin-erusin, the Romaniotes have adopted this odd custom as well."

They all stopped in unison at the gate to the synagogue. Maria looked at the vast crowd and took a deep breath before stepping inside. She had never seen so many Romaniotes in one place and felt rather uncomfortable. However, having to face members of the Catholic Church who were part of the Inquisition or leaving the only country she had ever known was far worse than this situation. So Maria held her head high, and not even her children knew of her fear.

They enjoyed the final moments of the ceremony and reverently listened to the reading of the ketubbah.

"How wonderful that the wife gets so much respect from her husband," commented Clara. Maria smiled at her niece. She was totally sure now that she and Teresa had done the right thing by moving here. Here Clara could have a secure future as well as a respected life, and all three children could live in safety.

Late in the evening the family returned home. The younger members didn't notice that Teresa seemingly hadn't moved from her place all day. Maria did, but made no comment in front of the other three. They were filled with excitement about the day and they fully told their grandmother about the ceremony, food, and entertainment. Clara was sure to mention the ketubbah.

Once their excitement had died down, Maria coaxed them to bed. Finally, they were asleep and Maria could fuss over Teresa, making her comfortable for the night. Now she had a chance to tell her mother-in-law her feelings about the day.

"It was a wonderful thing to be a part of," began Maria. Teresa nodded in agreement, too tired to speak. "We did the right thing you know," she added as she straightened Teresa's blankets. "Clara was most impressed with the idea of the ketubbah. She has a lot of confidence and will be fine. So will the boys. They are happy and safe and we must remember the sultan in our prayers." Maria whispered the last sentiment into Teresa's ear as she kissed her mother-in-law good night.

Glossary

abuela: Spanish, meaning "grandmother."

afikoman: Greek, meaning "dessert." It is used to refer to the final piece of matzah eaten after all the other food of the seder.

Ashkenazim: Jews who were originally from Germany and France, and their descendants. They spoke Judeo-German, the precursor to Yiddish.

bar: Hebrew, meaning "son of."

borekia: Pie, similar to an empañada or turnover. (A variation of the Turkish word "boerek.")

Converso: Term for Jews who were forced to convert to Christianity in the late Middle Ages during the Spanish Inquisition.

Dios mio: Spanish, meaning "My God."

Despoynida: Greek, meaning "Miss," used in reference to an unmarried woman.

entari: Sleeveless dress warn over the *kamiza* and *salvar*.

erusin: Hebrew, meaning "betrothal."

feraçe: Dust coat or lightweight full-length coat worn outside the house.

Glossary

fritadas: Ladino, referring to an omelette-type cake.

Gracias: Spanish, meaning "thank you."

Greco: Ladino, meaning "Greek." Used by the Sephardim as a derogatory term to refer to the Romaniote population.

halva: Sweet treat made from ground sesame seeds and either sugar or honey syrup. Often nuts or dried fruit are added.

hametz: Hebrew, referring to food containing some leavening agent, such as yeast.

hammam: Traditional public bath used in Turkey and other Middle Eastern countries. It included not only steam and cold water baths, but also cleansing baths and massages. It was the one place in Turkey where married women could meet outside of their homes.

haroset: Passover food symbolic of the mortar used by the Hebrew slaves to build the pyramids in Egypt.

harrisa: Pounded wheat and meat cooked into a porridge.

huppah: Canopy used during a Jewish wedding ceremony. It is said to symbolize the couple's new home, the community, and the separation of God above and people below.

imam: Arabic term used to refer to the leader of the prayer service.

kahal: Hebrew meaning "community," used to delineate a Jewish community that governs its internal affairs.

kamiza: Long-sleeved under garment worn over the *salvar* and under the *entari*.

kasher: Hebrew meaning "the act of koshering." (See kosher).

kassata: Cheese pastry or pie, similar to a quiche.

kehillah: Hebrew meaning "community." Used to delineate a Jewish community's governing group that interacts with the non-Jewish community.

ketubbah: Jewish marriage contract that details the obligations of the husband to his wife.

Kiddush: Hebrew, meaning "blessing." Used to refer to the blessing over the wine before a meal.

kiddushin: Hebrew, from the root "santicification." The ceremony where the betrothal is sanctified.

kookla: Greek, meaning "doll," which is often used as a pet name.

koritzi: Greek, meaning "girl."

kosher: Term used to describe foods that are acceptable according to Jewish dietary laws, and the method of preparing these foods.

Kyrio (pl. Kyries): Greek, meaning "mister."

Kyria: Greek, meaning "misses."

Glossary

Ladino: Judeo-Spanish language spoken by Sephardic Jews. It is written with Hebrew characters.

Manna: Greek, meaning "Mama."

Millet Bashi: Turkish, used to refer to the leader of the Jewish community appointed by the Muslim governor.

mikveh: Ritual bath used for purification purposes by both men and women.

Marrano: A historical term for a Spanish or Portuguese Jew who was forced to convert to Christianity in the late Middle Ages during the Spanish Inquisition. In more modern times, the term Converso, Crypto-Jew, or Anusim is preferred, as this has become derogatory.

Motzi: Blessing over bread

nalin: Footwear, similar to a clog.

nisuin: Hebrew, meaning "elevation." Often referred to as "home taking," where the bride is brought to the groom's home.

peçe: Black veil worn by Jewish women in public.

Provençal (pl. Provençals): People from what is now the Provençal region of France. In Thessaloniki, the term was used to refer to the Jews of that region.

Romaniote (pl. Romaniotes): Greek Jews who are thought to have lived in the territory of today's Greece for more than 2000 years.

salvar: Large loose pants, worn by men and women.

seder: Hebrew, meaning "order." Used to refer to the service celebrating the festival of Passover.

Sheva Brachot: The seven blessings recited during a Jewish wedding.

Señor: Spanish, meaning "Mister."

Señora: Spanish, meaning "Misses."

Señorita: Spanish meaning "Miss."

Sephardim: Jews who lived in Spain, Portugal, the Mediterranean Basin, North Africa, and the Middle East, and their descendants.

Shalom: Hebrew word that can mean "hello," "goodbye," or "peace."

Shavuot: The spring harvest festival that is one of the three pilgrimage festivals described in the Hebrew Scriptures. The other two are Passover and Sukkot.

Shuadit: Judeo-French language once spoken by the Jews of southern France. It is written with Hebrew characters.

stefana: Greek wedding crowns. In a custom adopted by the Romaniote community, stefana were used to signify that the bride and groom were creating a new kingdom or home.

tallit (pl. tallitot): Rectangular prayer shawl with fringes—traditionally worn by men.

tefillin: Pair of small black leather boxes with straps that contain pieces of parchment on which passages from the Torah are inscribed. Tefillin are attached to the forehead and arm of a man while he recites morning prayers.

Thea: Greek, meaning "aunt."

Tia: Spanish, meaning "aunt."

tik: The wooden or metal case in which Jews protect a Torah scroll in a Sephardic synagogue. Northern European Jews (Ashkenazim) cover their Torah with a mantle.

Torah: The first five books of the Bible: Genesis, Exodus, Leviticus, Numbers, and Deuteronomy. It also refers to a continuous parchment scroll on which the Hebrew words are written.

tzedakah: Charitable giving prescribed by Jewish law.

Yevanic: Judeo-Greek language, written with Hebrew characters, used by the Romaniotes. It was sometimes referred to as Romaniote; but to avoid confusion, only the term "Yevanic" is used in this book. Yevanic is no longer a spoken language.

Yaiya: Greek, meaning "grandmother."

Yiddish: The everyday Judeo-German language once spoken by many Ashkenazic Jews. It is written with Hebrew characters.

Yom Kippur: Day of Remembrance.